ROWAN COTTAGE

Recent Titles by Evelyn Hood

PEBBLES ON THE BEACH
A PRIDE OF SISTERS
THIS TIME NEXT YEAR
A WAKE FOR DONALD

THE OLIVE GROVE *

* *available from Severn House*

ROWAN COTTAGE

Evelyn Hood

This title first published in Great Britain 1999 by
SEVERN HOUSE PUBLISHERS LTD of
9–15 High Street, Sutton, Surrey SM1 1DF,
complete with new material from the author.
Originally published in 1983 by Mills & Boon under the title
Listen With Your Heart and pseudonym of *Elizabeth A. Webster.*
First published in the USA 1999 by
SEVERN HOUSE PUBLISHERS INC., of
595 Madison Avenue, New York, NY 10022.

British Library Cataloguing in Publication Data

Hood, Evelyn, 1936-
      Rowan Cottage
      1.   Love stories
      1.   Title II. Webster, Elizabeth A., 1936-. Listen with your heart
      823.9'14 [F]

      ISBN 0-7278-2299-3

Printed and bound in Great Britain by
MPG Books Ltd, Bodmin, Cornwall.

Author's Note

Atmosphere has a lot to do with fiction writing, and *Rowan Cottage* came into my mind almost fully-fledged during a brief three-hour visit to the beautiful Scottish border town of Dumfries. Like most very old towns or cities it is steeped in history, as well as being set in magnificent countryside.

In the past, communities on both sides of the Scottish-English borders were given to raiding each other, stealing cattle and on occasion, womenfolk. There must be many men such as Adam Brodie, the lawyer in the book, who are descended from families of Border raiders or "reivers". The keenest and strongest form of conflict is not between two people, but is to be found within one person forced to choose between desire and duty, and to tone down the hot-blooded instincts men such as Adam might find it hard to do.

As for love – it is one of the strongest, most powerful emotions known to the human race and it is to be found, in one form or another, in most writings.

Add an inherited cottage, a determined young woman, some antique jewellery, and the result is a story which I hope you will enjoy.

Evelyn Hood January 1999.

CHAPTER ONE

'AND just what the blazes do you think you're doing here?'

Jessica spun round, choking back a gasp of fright, as the deep voice cut through the cottage. Startled, she backed into the dimly lit area in the hall, staring at the figure that almost filled the open front door. A moment earlier that door had framed a sunny garden, trees beyond, and blue sky.

The tall figure moved forward to stand over her, a man with angry brown eyes and an arrogant note in his voice as he challenged again, 'Well? What are you doing in this cottage?'

As the shock of his sudden appearance ebbed away, a wave of anger moved in to take its place, and Jessica found her voice. 'I could ask you the same question!' she snapped at him.

'You could—but you won't. I happen to live in this area. I know that Rowan Cottage is empty at the moment. You're the stranger, not me, so I want to know what you're doing poking round the place. And how you got in. Through a window?'

Colour burned Jessica's face, and she drew herself up to her full height. Even at that, the stranger was at least a head taller than she was and his broad shoulders seemed to pin her into the corner of the hall, blocking her escape route

5

6

to the open door. Not that she wanted to escape—she was too angry to think of it.

'Of course I didn't come in through a window! What do you take me for—a burglar? Do I look like one, for heaven's sake?'

The brown eyes took time to sweep over her, studying her untidy fair hair, her flushed cheeks, the neat burgundy-coloured suit, the high-heeled shoes.

'No, you don't look like a burglar,' he admitted at last, though his eyes remained cold and watchful, and there was no change in his even voice with its Scottish accent.

Jessica tilted her chin defiantly. 'Well, you do!' It was her turn now to run her gaze over him, and she did so deliberately, taking in the brown windswept hair, the square face that looked as though it never smiled, the russet sweater and black jeans. 'How do I know that you live in the area? Have you any identification with you?'

Dark eyebrows shot up, and he was suddenly more human as he stared at her, startled by her attack. 'You mean that you—now I've heard everything!' he exploded. 'Look here, young lady——'

'You haven't heard everything. You haven't heard me threatening to sue you for trespass if you don't get out of here right now!'

'You can't sue someone for trespass in Scotland,' he told her promptly, side-tracked.

'Well—whatever I can sue you for. I'm sure there must be something! Just get out of my house—now!'

He blinked down at her. 'Your house? But——'

'My house,' Jessica repeated firmly. She hadn't completed her first year as a teacher without learning something herself. She adopted the decisive voice that had quelled a classroom full of high-spirited youngsters more than once. 'So, if you don't mind, I'd like you to leave, right now!'

As he showed no signs of moving, she pushed past him and went to the open door.

'You mean that you're Miss Ogilvie's great-niece?'

'You've heard about me?' Jessica supposed that everyone in the village must have heard of her inheritance. Great-aunt Kate had lived in Rowan Cottage for forty years, and no doubt the local people were eager to know who she had left it to. The stranger certainly seemed to be taken aback by her news.

'But you weren't supposed to arrive here until next week.'

'I decided to travel up from England earlier than planned. And I got the keys from the lawyer's secretary.' She took them from her pocket and flourished them. 'And I have made an appointment to see the lawyer tomorrow to put things on a legal footing. I don't know why I feel that I have to explain my actions to you, but there it is. I did not have to come in through a window, and this is my cottage. You are the intruder—not me.'

The man had the grace to look slightly embarrassed. 'Look, I'd better explain——' he began, and took a step towards her.

Just then something hit Jessica violently in the back, and before she could do more than give a squeak of outraged protest, she had been propelled across the tiny hallway and into the intruder's arms.

If he hadn't caught her, she would have fallen. For a few bewildered seconds she was held close to him, her face buried in the soft russet sweater. Something heavy hit the back of her legs, and she tightened her own grasp round a strong, steady body, aware, even in her confusion, of the smell of fresh country air rather than the usual whiff of aftershave.

'Toby!' a deep voice rumbled through the hard chest beneath her cheek. 'Toby—get down at once—down!' Then Jessica was held back at arm's length and the brown eyes, concerned now, studied her. 'Are you all right?'

'I—I think so. What on earth——?' She stepped out of his grasp, pushing the hair from her eyes, brushing down her skirt, looking in dismay at laddered stockings.

'It's my fault,' the stranger said, and she saw that he had grabbed at a half-grown black Labrador's collar. 'Toby's still at the puppy stage, and he hasn't fully learned not to throw himself at people. I'll deal with you later, Toby,' he added severely to the dog, and it licked apologetically at his hand.

'It was hardly the dog's fault—he can't help it if he's not trained properly!'

Anger tightened the man's face, driving the hint of warmth from his eyes. 'I assure you,

Miss Taylor, that I do know how to train a dog!'

'Do you? I believe in training by example,' Jessica snapped back. She was tired after travelling for two days, she was suddenly furious with him for spoiling her excitement and delight with the cottage. The dog was the last straw. 'You can hardly punish the animal for barging into my house uninvited. He was merely copying his master's behaviour. So far, you haven't knocked me down, but I'm sure you'll get round to it, given time!'

'For heaven's sake——' he began, straightening up to face her and relaxing his grip on the dog's collar. Toby immediately wriggled loose, brushing against a small table and knocking an ornament over. It was the last straw.

'Go away!'

'Look, Miss Tay——'

'Just—go away! And take your dog with you!' she almost shouted at him. 'And don't bother coming back to apologise!'

He hesitated, took one step towards her, then shrugged and went out without another word. Jessica slammed the front door shut behind them, just in case they turned back, and then she went into the sitting-room and watched through the window as they went down the path. The man carefully latched the gate behind himself, his mouth tight. Then he turned and walked down the road without a backward glance, Toby gambolling in front of him. A full-grown Labrador, as black as Toby, rose from the grassy verge and greeted the man sedately, then trotted by his side as he moved out of sight with the long, relaxed strides of a countryman.

Jessica went upstairs and studied her face in the bathroom mirror. Her hair, which had once been pinned neatly at the back of her head, hung in fair tendrils round a flushed face. She looked hot and bad-tempered and exhausted, and she realised that there was no danger of the stranger wanting to come back to apologise. She looked thoroughly unpleasant, and he was probably dismayed by the prospect of a virago like her living in the area.

She bathed her face in cold water, loosened her hair and combed it out so that it swung round her face. She put on some make-up, and began to feel calmer. In the kitchen she foraged in cupboards and was delighted to find that there was coffee and sugar as well as a good store of tins and packets. She made coffee, poured it into a pretty flowered mug, and perched on a high stool so that she could look out at the neat, colourful back garden as she drank the hot, reviving liquid.

She had hoped to find a peaceful holiday in the gentle, rolling hills of the Scottish Borders, but, so far, she told herself ruefully, she hadn't done well. With any luck, the rest of the community would prove to be more pleasant than the man who had burst in on her as she was exploring the cottage.

She pushed him to the back of her mind, concentrating on the excitement of seeing Rowan Cottage for the first time, unlocking the door and walking into the little house that had been left to her by Great-aunt Kate Ogilvie. Jessica had intended to spend her summer holiday with her parents in Spain, where her father was working for several months, but the lawyer's letter informing her briskly that Miss Ogilvie had willed Rowan Cottage to her great-niece had changed everything. Jessica had written to her parents, telling them that she intended to go to Scotland and spend a week or two in the cottage, unwinding after a busy school year and deciding what to do with her inheritance, before flying out to Spain. She had written to the lawyer, notifying him of her intention to arrive in Broominch ten days after the school closed. But, on an impulse, she had packed her things and left, heading North almost as soon as she had wiped the chalk from her fingers, anxious to get away from her small flat and her ordinary, routine life.

And she had done the right thing, she knew that now. She rinsed the empty mug, left it on the draining board, and wandered into the sitting-room. Rowan Cottage was very small, but Great-aunt Kate had obviously loved it. The furniture was all old, but well cared for. Polished wood glowed, the rugs and chairs were in soft pastel shades, and brasses winked from the walls. There was a restful air about the place that answered a need in Jessica's heart. Her first teaching year had been exhilarating, but tiring. She was by nature a loner, and Broominch and its surrounding countryside was just what she needed.

Then the peaceful scene before her faded, to be replaced by memories of a deep voice with an attractive Scottish accent, untidy brown hair with gold glints in it, a firm mouth, and cool brown eyes, darkening in sudden anger. Jessica sensed a rush of irritation. Why had he come barging in when she was exploring the cottage—her cottage? Why did he and his dog have to spoil her first precious moments, moments when she had been trying to capture some understanding of Great-aunt Kate, that elusive shadow? She recalled the well-shaped mouth, and realised that he hadn't smiled once. She didn't trust people who couldn't smile. And yet—he looked as though he just might, in the right situation.

She ran her fingers over the smooth golden wood of the round table, and she knew that the table should have a bowl of flowers on it. Her grey eyes sparkled with triumph as she found the bowl—earthenware, finished in deep blue—in the dresser by the wall. Perhaps Kate Ogilvie and Jessica Taylor had something in common, after all.

Scissors waited for her in a drawer in the kitchen. Evening was approaching as Jessica went out to the front garden, and the air was cool and soft against her face. She cut bunches of small golden roses from a bush near the gate, and took a long time to arrange them. The result was worth the effort, for the table's surface reflected the blue bowl and yellow roses perfectly, and the room was already beginning to carry a trace of the flowers' soft fragrance.

She yawned, rubbing aching eyes, and realised that she was very tired. She was not used to driving long distances, and excitement had kept her awake for most of the time during her overnight stop. Reluctantly, she took one more look around the cottage and left, noting as she locked the door and walked to the gate that the garden had been well tended recently. The flower beds were weed-free, and the hedge neatly trimmed. Somebody must have been working in it, and no doubt had presented a bill for the work to the lawyer.

As she turned her small yellow car and headed for the village hotel, she looked back at Rowan Cottage. It was tucked into a corner of land beside the road, with no neighbours, and yet it didn't look like a solitary place. It had an air of contentment, as though it enjoyed being alone. An air, Jessica decided as she turned the corner and the cottage was lost to view, that was very like hers, and suited her well. She had intended to make plans to sell the cottage at once, as her own life was firmly rooted in England, but now she was not so sure.

As she was falling asleep in her room an hour or so later, she remembered that the intruder had called her by name. But then, everyone in Broominch would know everyone else's business. It was a small place. They would all be expecting her, wondering what she was like and what she planned to do with Rowan Cottage.

She awoke to a blue sky, and planned her day over a leisurely breakfast. School seemed very far away. She would have liked to hurry back to the cottage, but she had made an appointment with Mr Brodie, her great-aunt's lawyer, for early afternoon. His office was in the nearby town, and it seemed more sensible to have a look around the place before going to see him.

After considerable thought she changed from her jeans and shirt into something more in keeping with a visit to a lawyer. She selected a dark blue pleated skirt, teamed it with a rose-pink blouse, brushed her long fair hair back and tied it loosely with a chiffon scarf that matched the blouse. Pink lipstick and a touch of blue eye-shadow to emphasise her large grey eyes, her best feature, completed her preparations, and she was soon driving along a country road, beneath an archway of green.

There was a car-park situated beside the river that ran through the older part of the Border town. Jessica bought a street map, and spent the rest of the morning wandering happily through narrow streets bright with shops and packed with local people and holiday-makers. She had some lunch in a small restaurant near the river, then walked across the old stone bridge, pausing half-way to dream in the sun, her arms resting on the parapet. A family of swans glided smoothly out from under the bridge, the last cygnet scurrying along in an effort to catch up, the parents snowy white, disdainful. A fish jumped in the still pool further down, beneath a small weir, its silvery body catching the sun as it plopped back into the cool depths. From where Jessica stood, the old

town was a pattern of soft grey shades, the houses
jostling each other in friendly harmony. Many of
them had tiny windows and elegant crow-stepped
gables. Although she had never been in the
district before, Jessica felt as though she was in
familiar surroundings. The fact that she knew
nobody in the town didn't bother her one bit.
She felt safe, in tune with the river and the
ancient bridge and the soft stone-grey patterns of
the houses.

She glanced at her watch and was surprised
to find that she had dreamed an hour away. Mr
Brodie's office wasn't far from the river, and
she reached it in good time, climbing the
narrow stairs in the old building and entering
the small reception area as a distant clock struck
the hour.

The secretary who had handed the keys of
Rowan Cottage to her on the previous afternoon
beamed as Jessica went in. 'There you are, Miss
Taylor. Did you find the cottage yesterday?'

'Yes, I did. It's beautiful.'

'Aye, I always thought myself that it was one of
the nicest cottages in the village,' the woman said
in her soft Scottish voice. 'I'll just go and tell Mr
Brodie you're here.'

Jessica waited in the plain, serviceable reception
area. Obviously Mr Brodie had a business of long
standing, and felt no need to modernise the
premises, she thought idly.

'Can you give him a moment?' the secretary
came back. 'He's been held up—he's just getting
Miss Ogilvie's papers together.'

'Has Mr Brodie been my great-aunt's lawyer for long?'

'Since ever she came to Broominch, I think. And that must be about forty years ago. But——' a buzzer sounded, and she stood up. 'I'll take you along to his office.'

Jessica followed her into a short dark hallway she had not been in on her first brief visit. The woman opened a door, and dazzling light blinded Jessica for a moment as she stepped forward. It came from two large windows overlooking the river, and they received the full force of the sun. She turned from the glare, studying the rest of the room until her eyes got used to the sunlight after the neon-lit reception area and the dim corridor. There were filing cabinets, a few comfortable-looking chairs, and a huge desk piled high with papers that overflowed on to the floor and the chairs. The secretary scooped a bundle of them from one chair and announced:

'Here's Miss Taylor——'

It was little wonder, Jessica thought as she moved further into the room, that Mr Brodie had had to hunt for the Ogilvie papers.

Then the man who had been silhouetted against one window as he looked down at the river, turned. 'Good afternoon, Miss Taylor.'

'Good——' She stopped as her hand disappeared into a firm clasp. Her eyes widened as she looked up into the lawyer's face. His brown hair was neatly brushed back, and he was wearing a white shirt, dark tie and grey suit, beautifully cut. But there was no mistaking that deep voice, or the steady brown eyes, still without the trace of a smile.

'You're surprised, Miss Taylor—but then, I forgot to introduce myself yesterday,' he said smoothly. 'Or should I say, you never gave me the chance. Will you take a seat?'

'You two know each other?' the secretary asked with interest.

'You could say so. Mebbe you could make some coffee for us, Morag——?' He raised an eyebrow at her, and she left, putting the papers she held on the top of a cabinet as she went out. The lawyer settled his tall frame into the swivel chair behind the desk, his large hands gathering up papers with practised ease.

'Now, Miss Taylor, there are some documents for you to sign, and I have an inventory of the contents of Rowan Cottage here. Did you make a list of the contents when you were there yesterday?'

'I was interrupted,' she said sweetly, determined to get some response from him. He merely looked thoughtfully at her. 'I'm sorry, I should have asked—you're none the worse for your meeting with Toby, I hope?'

'I recovered. You can deduct the cost of a new pair of stockings from your bill.'

For a moment, one corner of his mouth quirked, but he lowered his head quickly over the papers, saying evenly, 'I'll make a note of it. I'll have to go out to the cottage with you and check the inventory. It was made out as soon as——'
He looked up again, stopped talking, and Jessica realised that she had been staring.

'Are you listening, Miss Taylor?'

'I'm sorry—it's just that I had expected someone——'

'Older.' He finished the sentence for her. 'People do. They forget that lawyers can start practising before they become white-haired.'

She flushed at the irony in his voice. 'I understood that this firm had represented my great-aunt for forty years, and I took it for granted that her lawyer would be an older man.'

'My father, James Brodie, was your aunt's lawyer until he retired last year. I am Adam Brodie, I am thirty-three years old, and I run the firm now,' he explained patiently, and she felt the flush deepen under his cool scrutiny. 'Now, if you would just let me explain these documents——'

When the coffee arrived Jessica was trying to make some sense out of the papers strewn across the desk. She sipped the hot liquid thankfully, glad of a respite, but the man on the other side of the huge desk left his coffee to cool while he worked on, dark brows knotted in concentration.

'We should discuss the future of Rowan Cottage as well,' he said finally. 'The contents of the place are quite valuable, as you probably realised. Good antique furniture, some very nice pieces of china and glass. They should bring you a tidy sum, and the cottage itself is worth a good price. As a matter of fact, I already have a buyer who is very interested, and willing to pay the full market value.'

'A buyer? But I haven't made up my mind what to do with the cottage!'

He got to his feet, walked to the window, then turned and looked down at her. She couldn't see his face, which was in shadow, but she could tell by his voice that he was impatient with her.

'Miss Taylor, I understand that you are a teacher, and that you live and work in England. You'll have no use for a cottage in the South of Scotland, surely!'

The coffee cup rattled sharply back on to its saucer and Jessica put it down.

'I'd like to make up my own mind about Rowan Cottage's future.'

He moved to a cabinet in the corner, opened and shut a dawer, then sat down at his desk again. The impatience had become thinly-veiled irritation.

'You're not planning to use it as a holiday home, I hope? It's a fine place, and I'd not like to think of it being used as the mood takes you, and left empty for most of the year. It deserves a better future than that!'

The arrogance of the man almost choked Jessica. He had succeeded, in one way and another, in ruining her pleasure in her inheritance.

'Now just a minute, Mr Brodie, I think that the future of Rowan Cottage is my concern, not yours. After all, I do own it—or are you going to tell me I'm wrong about that, too?'

Their eyes locked, stormy grey meeting cold brown and both pairs refused to give way. Then Adam Brodie drew a deep breath.

'You own the cottage and, of course, it is up to you to decide what you wish to do with it,' he said levelly. 'But as your lawyer——'

'As my lawyer, you should offer me assistance!' she snapped at him. 'You're not supposed to make decisions for me. I'm well aware, Mr Brodie, that I'm not nearly as clever as you are. I only teach infant classes—although you'll be surprised to hear that I do it rather well. And you probably think that at twenty-two I'm too young to own property. But I have lived alone for the past three years, and I have managed, so far, to cope with my own life!'

There was a short pause then Adam Brodie, his face expressionless, said, 'I happen to have a free afternoon. I could take you to the cottage now to check the inventory.'

She almost refused, almost walked out there and then, but realised just in time that she would have to work with him until such time as the legal business was finished.

'My car's parked by the river,' she said stiffly. 'I'll meet you at the cottage.'

He unfolded himself from the chair in a smooth, easy movement, crossed the room with the same athletic stride she had seen on the previous afternoon, and opened the door for her. 'We'll go in my car,' he said as though daring her to argue, and she walked meekly ahead of him into the corridor.

As she was about to get into the sleek black car parked at the back of his office, she hesitated and looked up at him. 'Mr Brodie—do you ever smile?'

The question caught him unawares. His dark eyes widened briefly, the corner of his mouth quivered, then firmed again. 'I'm not paid to smile, Miss Taylor,' he told her.

They drove to the cottage without speaking to each other. As he turned the car into the street, Adam Brodie flicked a button on the dash, and started a Neil Diamond tape which filled the silence pleasantly. Jessica recalled that her closest friend, Elizabeth, had once remarked that nobody who liked Neil Diamond could be all bad. She made a mental note, glancing at Adam Brodie's strong, serious profile, to tell Elizabeth that she was wrong.

Her heart rose as soon as the cottage came into view. All at once she hated the thought of letting the house go—and yet the man beside her was right, there was no question of her being able to keep it when her career was in England.

Adam drove the car into the grassy area by the side of the garden with an ease that must have been born of practice. Jessica unclipped her seat-belt and got out before he could open the passenger door for her. She hurried up the path and opened the door—and Rowan Cottage welcomed her with the same peaceful, un-surprised air she had found on her first visit. Waiting for Adam, she noticed how out of place he looked in his town suit. He had fitted the place very well in his sweater and jeans, his two dogs by his side and his hair ruffled by the breeze.

The tight roses she had put on the table the

day before had opened out, and their scent filled the sitting-room. Adam's brows rose when he followed her into the room.

'I cut them last night, from the garden. The room seemed to need flowers.'

'Miss Ogilvie always had roses there in the summer.'

'I thought she did.' Relaxed now that she was back in Rowan Cottage, she smiled at him, but the smile was not returned. Instead he stood looking at her thoughtfully, as though seeing her anew against the background of the cottage. Then he blinked and turned towards the table, putting his brief-case down, taking lists from it.

'Well—we'd better get on with this inventory.'

It seemed endless. Every piece of furniture, every ornament and picture, had to be checked. While Adam Brodie went about the task with a formal, impersonal air, Jessica took the opportunity to absorb the cottage more thoroughly than she had been able to before. She slowly started to picture Great-aunt Kate there, collecting and caring for her lovely furniture, lovingly placing each piece of china, hanging each picture.

'I wish I had known her.'

'What did you say?' Adam looked up from his list as though he had forgotten Jessica existed.

'Great-aunt Kate. I wish I had known her. I only met her when she came to England, you see. She always seemed—remote.'

He shook his head firmly. 'She was never remote. You saw her out of her surroundings.'

They had reached the bedroom, and Jessica sat on a tapestry chair by the window. 'Did you know her well?'

'Yes. She visited my father's house quite often.'

'Tell me about her.'

He frowned, hesitated, seemed about to shake his head, then said slowly, 'Well—she was a gentle person. She had a sense of humour, and a great love of the countryside.' He stared beyond Jessica's head, out of the window. 'People liked her. People—miss her.'

For that moment, he looked like a real person. There was a tenderness in his face that softened the stern lines. His eyes were dreamy, warm—then the moment passed and he looked at Jessica, the businessman again. 'She was a good client,' he said formally. 'Now, shall we get on?'

At last they were finished. In the sitting-room again, Jessica signed the inventory and Adam witnessed it in a clear, firm hand. 'That's that.'

'I wish I could offer you something to drink,' she said on an impulse. 'After all, you are my first visitor—for the second time. But I don't think——'

'You weren't paying attention when we checked the place out,' he said reprovingly, turning to the lovely dresser where Kate Ogilvie's china was stored. He opened a door, reached in, and brought out a bottle and two delicate crystal glasses. 'Miss Ogilvie always offered her visitors a glass of the very best sherry.' He opened the bottle, half filled the glasses with amber-coloured liquid, and brought them to Jessica as she stood by the window.

'To Rowan Cottage—its past, and its future.' She raised her glass, and after giving her another of his long, searching looks, he did the same.

'Who's been tending the garden?' she remembered to ask as they stood drinking their sherry.

'As Miss Ogilvie's lawyer, I saw to it that the garden was looked after.' He moved behind her to look out of the window, and she was aware of his quiet strength close by, his deep voice beside her ear.

'I'll have to pay the gardener.'

'I've seen to that.'

Being so close to him disturbed her, for some reason. She moved away, towards the kitchen. 'I'll rinse out the glasses.'

The kitchen was tiny when he followed her into it and put his own glass down by the sink. 'There's still the garden shed to be checked out. I forgot about it.'

'You start on it and I'll come out when I've seen to the glasses.'

He unlocked the back door, and she watched from the window as he crossed the small lawn. The shed stood in the shelter of a willow tree at the other side of the lawn. Beyond that was a wall of warm red brick, separating the garden from the field beyond. Adam opened the shed door with a key he had lifted from a hook in the kitchen and went in, stooping to get under the lintel.

Jessica rinsed the glasses, dried them and polished them, then put them back in the dresser. As she closed the door footsteps sounded on the flagged front path and someone tapped on the open door.

'Adam?' It was a girl's voice, musical but impatient. The voice of someone used to getting an instant response. Jessica went into the hall just as the girl in the doorway stepped forward. 'Adam, I—oh! You must be the new owner.'

Vivid blue eyes swept over Jessica. The newcomer was a girl of about her own age. She wore a shirt and riding jodhpurs and her glossy black hair was shoulder-length.

'I was passing when I saw Adam's car. I didn't realise that you'd arrived. Where's Adam?'

Her imperious manner stung colour into Jessica's cheeks.

'He's in the garden.'

'He's told you, I suppose? That I want the cottage, I mean. You'll be glad to get it off your hands without any hassle.'

She would have walked into the sitting-room, but Jessica stayed where she was, barring the way. 'No, he didn't tell me.'

'Really?' The girl looked annoyed. 'He probably hasn't had time. Well, since I'm here we can decide the whole thing right now, get it over with.'

'Look——' Jessica tried not to let anger creep into her voice. It seemed to her that everyone who walked into Rowan Cottage brought trouble. And she was tired of the way people in

Broominch took it for granted that she would go along with their plans.

But the newcomer had lost interest in Jessica. Her eyes had moved to a spot beyond and above Jessica, and her full lips had curved into a smile. Jessica swung round and saw that Adam Brodie was standing in the doorway just behind her, hair slightly rumpled from his visit to the shed, a smear of oil on one cheek giving him a slightly endearing look.

'Adam!' the girl said, haughty impatience swept sway. 'Darling—there you are!'

And she brushed past Jessica, reached up to put her arms about Adam Brodie's neck, and kissed him lightly, but possessively, on the lips.

CHAPTER TWO

IsHBEL STEVENSON was beautiful. She was slim, shapely, immaculate in a white shirt tucked into well-cut jodhpurs. A blue scarf, the exact colour of her eyes, was knotted carelessly at her throat. From the top of her shining black head to the toes of her expensive riding boots she indicated money, and all the confidence that went with it.

Ishbel Stevenson owned Adam Brodie, and made sure that Jessica knew it. She stood in the little sitting-room at Rowan Cottage, her arm linked through his, studying Jessica with ill-concealed annoyance. Because Ishbel Stevenson, Jessica realised with a stab of pleasure, didn't own Rowan Cottage, and she wanted to. Some perverse streak that Jessica hadn't even known she possessed rose up in her at the other girl's cool assumption that the cottage would be sold to her.

'After all,' Ishbel was saying, 'the land round here all belongs to the original farm, and it would be nice to get it back in the family. Now that Miss Ogilvie's gone, it's the ideal time for me to put in my bid. You'll do well out of it financially, I can assure you of that.'

'Ishbel,' Adam Brodie drew away from her, a slight frown furrowing his forehead, 'I think that the future of the cottage should be discussed in my office, not here.'

She laughed. 'Darling, you're being very legal today, aren't you? Why shouldn't we sort it out now, since—Jessica—is here. Then she can get back home. I'm sure she doesn't want to stay in Broominch any longer than she has to.'

'I'm in no hurry. I like this part of the world,' Jessica said quietly. 'And I can't think why you should want Rowan Cottage.'

'I told you, it's on our land——'

'It was, until your grandfather sold it to Miss Ogilvie.'

'You're being legal again, Adam.' There was a hard note in the girl's lovely voice, but Adam seemed unaware of it as he busied himself with his brief-case. 'The land did belong to my family, and my mother would have liked it back, you know that. This used to be a farmhand's cottage, you see,' she explained to Jessica.

'And you need it for that purpose again?'

'Good heavens, no!' Ishbel was amused. 'The farmland has been sold—most of it. I want the cottage for myself. I need a place of my own, away from the main house. Somewhere where I could entertain my friends——' she let the words hang in the rose-scented air, her eyes fixed on Adam Brodie's broad back, and Jessica knew who Ishbel was anxious to entertain in the privacy of her own home.

'I see.'

He straightened from the table, where he had finished putting papers into his brief-case. 'See what, Miss Taylor?'

'I see that the disposal of the cottage was decided before I set foot in Broominch.'

'Oh—really!' Ishbel said impatiently, while Adam Brodie's frown returned. 'Miss Taylor, I think you're jumping to conclusions. And as for you, Ishbel—I think you're talking out of turn. I have to get back to the office, so——'

'I think that if anyone is jumping to conclusions, it's Miss Stevenson. Rowan Cottage is not for sale.'

They stared at her, then at each other; Adam surprised, Ishbel angry. Then Ishbel said, 'You can't mean that you intend to live here?'

'Why not?'

'But—Adam, tell her how ridiculous the whole idea is——'

'My great-aunt lived here for forty years—there's no reason why I shouldn't do so.' Jessica couldn't believe that the words came from her own lips. She had had no thought of staying in Broominch until Ishbel's insolence pushed her into making the decision. She was as staggered by her own news as the others were.

Ishbel stepped forward. 'Miss Ogilvie did live here for a long time, but that's different. She had a reason. She was——'

'Ishbel!' Adam's voice cracked like a whip across her words, and she subsided. He looked angry as he put his hand on her arm. 'Ishbel, there is no sense in going on with the discussion at present. Please leave things to me!'

She was about to argue, then she gave in suddenly, putting her hand over his. 'If you insist, Adam.'

'I do insist.' His voice was cool. 'And now I'm
going back to town. Miss Taylor, I'll drive you
back to the car-park.'

Ishbel turned to Jessica, her lovely face
suddenly lit by a warm smile. 'I'm sorry, Jessica.
I spoke without stopping to think. Adam's
right—I should count ten before I open my
mouth.'

'You're too used to getting your own way.' His
voice was still angry.

'That,' said Ishbel sweetly, linking her hand
through his arm again, 'is because I always do, in
the end.'

She and Adam waited at the gate while Jessica
locked the cottage door. When she walked down
the path Ishbel was springing nimbly into the
saddle of a chestnut horse which had been tied to
the gatepost.

'I'll see you tonight, Adam. Goodbye,
Jessica.'

He stood and watched as she walked the horse
to the end of the lane twenty yards from the
cottage gate. She turned and waved, then she
rode out of sight, up the lane.

He drove fast through the country lanes on the
way back, tooting the horn impatiently when he
found himself behind a tractor. The cumbersome
machine drew in to the side of the road and
Adam swung the car past, accelerating sharply.
Glancing at his profile, Jessica saw that he was
tense, locked in his own thoughts. She had plenty
to occupy her own mind—resentment at Ishbel's
attitude, anger over the way the other girl had

taken it for granted that the cottage should be sold to her, astonishment at her own bald announcement that Rowan Cottage was not going to be given up as easily as Ishbel thought. Like Adam Brodie, Jessica was not in the mood for conversation.

He pulled up beside her car and came round to open the passenger door. 'You weren't serious about keeping the cottage?' he asked abruptly when she was standing beside him.

Jessica tilted her chin so that she could look up at him. 'Of course I was. I've decided to move into it tomorrow.'

'But——'

'Is there any reason why I can't?'

'Well—no,' he admitted, frowning. 'But I do think that you——'

'I think someone's trying to attract your attention.' Jessica nodded at an elderly man who was making his way as quickly as he could, with the aid of a walking stick, towards them.

Adam swung round. 'Oh—it's my father,' he said, with little enthusiasm in his deep voice.

James Brodie was beaming when he reached them. 'Adam, I went to the office and Morag said you were at Rowan Cottage. Is this Miss Taylor?' He studied Jessica with interest. His son introduced them tersely, and Jessica was struck at once by the warmth of James's eyes as he took her hand in a firm grip.

'My dear, I have been looking forward to meeting you for the past two months.' His piercing grey eyes examined her face, and seemed to like what they saw. He nodded, and patted her hand before releasing it. 'Yes indeed, I have wanted to meet Kate Ogilvie's great-niece. Welcome to Rowan Cottage.'

It was the first time anyone had said that, and she felt an instant surge of affection for this charming old man who, she realised, resembled his son closely. James's hair was snowy white, but had the thickness and springiness of Adam's, and the same way of flopping over his forehead. He had a strong, well-shaped face with his son's firm mouth and direct look.

'I have to get back to the office,' Adam said with a hint of impatience.

'I'll come with you. There are things to be discussed. I hope you've invited Miss Taylor to the house as I asked, Adam?'

'I haven't had the opportunity,' his son said, but Jessica could tell by the brief look of annoyance that flashed into his dark eyes that he had had no intention of passing on the invitation.

'You will come to dinner, won't you, Miss Taylor? Tonight, if you like—no, Adam's going out tonight, aren't you, Adam?'

'You can hold a dinner party without me.'

'I would like you to be there. Tomorrow evening, Miss Taylor?'

'Jessica. And I'd love to have dinner with you tomorrow, thank you.' She should have refused, because it was clear to her that Adam didn't want her to go to his father's house. But she was still smarting from Ishbel's behaviour, and she was in no mood now to please Adam. His mouth tightened, but he said nothing.

'Adam will call for you. Seven o'clock at your hotel.'

'Seven o'clock will be fine—and I'll be at Rowan Cottage,' Jessica said sweetly to Adam. He nodded formally.

'At Rowan Cottage, then.'

She waited as he and his father got into the sleek black car, and watched as they drove away. Then she went back on to the old stone bridge. Below, the water was dappled by sunlight, the surface broken here and there by patches of weeds. The swans had gone, but a fish jumped as she leaned on the warm stone wall, the ripples of its leap spreading rapidly across the surface.

Jessica took a deep breath. 'Well, my girl,' she murmured to herself, 'it looks as though you've just burned your boats, doesn't it?'

A tremor of excitement mingled with fear fluttered through her, then she took herself to task. She had six weeks' holiday ahead of her, the flat in Middlesex could be left safely for that length of time, and she would write at once to her parents and her friends to let them know her plans. Then she would be free to get to know the cottage and Broominch, with at least four clear weeks before she had to begin making decisions. And she could certainly do with a quiet holiday, in any case.

After dinner she wrote letters, made lists of food to be bought, and made arrangements to leave the hotel on the following morning. She went out and posted the letters, then wandered for a while round the village in the dusk. When she returned to the hotel its lights were on, and a cheerful buzz of voices came from the lounge bar. Jessica hesitated. She had just taken an important step, she had made a lot of decisions that day, and was about to start a new, if temporary, way of life in a few hours' time. Surely it was an occasion to celebrate with one drink before bedtime? She moved forward, then stopped, her hand on the handle of the glass door which led into the bar from the foyer.

Directly ahead of her in the crowded room was a table. A group of people were crowded round it, including Adam Brodie and Ishbel Stevenson. Adam was listening intently to a man seated across the table from him. By his side Ishbel, elegant in a crimson dress, had one hand laid lightly on Adam's arm.

As Jessica watched, Adam broke into a gale of laughter, his head thrown back, his dark eyes crinkled with amusement. He looked, all at once, like a man who was used to laughter, quite unlike the serious lawyer who had told her 'I am not paid to smile'.

Ishbel said something and Adam, still grinning, answered her. He wore a white polo-necked sweater under an open brown jacket, and his hair fell over his forehead. As she spoke, Ishbel reached up and smoothed the untidy lock of hair back from his face.

Jessica's fingers fell away from the door handle. She moved away quickly, afraid that he might look up and see her there, watching him.

But he was too absorbed in his friends, and in Ishbel, to notice the movement behind the glass door opposite. Jessica turned towards the stairs, giving up the idea of a celebration drink.

As she returned to her room she felt lonely for the first time in her life. It was not a pleasant sensation.

The feeling of despondency had vanished when she woke up the next morning and remembered that she was moving to Rowan Cottage. Briefly, as she breakfasted, packed and shopped, she recalled the picture in the bar on the previous evening, but it was easy to dismiss it from her mind. The sight of the happy crowd, she now felt, had reminded her that her own friends were in England, far away. But she would meet new friends in Broominch. She had always found it easy to get to know people although she preferred her own company quite often. And she knew that she was going to enjoy living in Rowan Cottage. She was eager to learn something about Great-aunt Kate during the summer, and perhaps, living in new surroundings, she would learn something about herself.

The cottage waited for her, the garden bright, the rooms dappled with sunlight and serenely welcoming as she unlocked the front door.

The day seemed to fly past. Jessica unpacked the car, arranged her clothes in Great-aunt Kate's wardrobe, filled the food cupboards in the kitchen, and installed her sponge bag and toothbrush in the bathroom. She made a light lunch and took it into the back garden. Some birds arrived on the little lawn almost at once, eyeing her with interest and accepting the crumbs she threw. Obviously they had been used to being fed on that lawn. Later, Jessica swept and dusted the cottage, aired sheets and blankets, and cut more flowers to fill the vases she found in a kitchen cupboard.

There was not much to be done, but enough to keep her occupied. When the sheets were brought in again, sweet-smelling and fresh, she made up her bed and explored the garden shed. Baskets, twine, gardening tools and canes were all there, neatly stacked against the walls or arranged on shelves. Jessica was used to working in her parents' garden and missed it now that they were abroad and she was in a flat. She lifted a trowel, hefted it thoughtfully in her hand, and couldn't resist the urge to start working on one of the flower beds flanking the lawn.

The sun was going down and she was happily engrossed in her work when she suddenly realised that a pair of black polished shoes had moved into her line of vision as she knelt on a path. Startled, she looked up, her eyes travelling from the shoes to a pair of grey trousers, a grey jacket, a strong chin with just the hint of a cleft, an unsmiling mouth, brown eyes . . .

'Oh—hello.' She sat back on her heels and rubbed one hand across her face, smearing a trail of earth across her cheek. 'I didn't hear you arriving.'

'So I gather.' Adam Brodie eyed the scarf she had tied over her hair, the dirty face, the trowel in one grimy hand, then glanced down at the handsome watch on his wrist. 'It's—er—it's seven o'clock.'

'My goodness, is it? I didn't realise that—oh!' She jumped to her feet, horrified. 'Seven o'clock? That's when you were going to——'

'—to take you to my father's house for dinner,' he finished the sentence for her patiently, as though she was a rather ignorant child. 'Exactly.'

'Oh. Well——' she looked down at herself, then back up at him. 'I'm so sorry. I didn't realise what time it was. I'm not ready.'

He studied the navy shirt, rumpled and grubby, the faded blue jeans that she loved dearly but could only wear when there was nobody around to see how shabby they were, the scarf with tendrils of fair hair escaping from it. His mouth trembled, and was instantly stilled.

'I can see that.'

Jessica felt the colour rise into her face. He didn't have to be so sarcastic.

'I can be ready in five minutes—really. Well, ten minutes.'

'Or I could explain to my father that something unavoidable has cropped up, and give your apologies,' he offered quickly.

'Oh no—no! I really do want to go and have dinner with him—with both of you. It's just——' She made to hand him the trowel, then pulled it back in confusion. 'Sorry—you'd better not come too near me just now with that lovely suit on. I could ruin it.'

'Yes,' Adam agreed, and stepped back. Anger

flared in Jessica as she saw the look in his eyes.

'Obviously,' she said with as much ice in her voice as she could manage, 'you're not a gardener. Gardening is a wonderful hobby, and very absorbing.' Then, as he said nothing, but stood there, looking down on her, her poise broke. 'Look—go in and get yourself a drink. I'll be ready in ten minutes,' she gabbled, and fled past him into the house.

In front of the full-length mirror in the bedroom she looked at herself, and could have wept, if she had had the time for such self-indulgence. Her face was dirty, her hair straggled out from under the bright scarf, her shirt hung untidily over her appalling jeans, and she wore a pair of old sandals on her otherwise bare feet. She looked like a teen-age drop-out, and certainly not like an adult capable of making her own decisions about Rowan Cottage or anything else.

Frantically, she ran a bath, knotted her hair on top of her head, peeled off the grubby clothes and dropped them on the floor, and tossed a handful of bath-salts into the warm water. She bathed hurriedly, and was soon towelling herself. She slipped into clean underwear and selected a pale green dress in a silky material, with a round neck, tiered skirt, and wide sleeves caught just below the elbows. White sandals, lipstick and a touch of light perfume made up the outfit, and after brushing her hair until it curled in a soft, shining mass about her face, she was ready. Picking up a white shawl, she hurried downstairs to find Adam in the sitting-room, a book in his hand.

He looked up with surprise when she went in; then the look softened momentarily into admiration.

'Ready.'

He put the book away. 'Twenty minutes—not bad, considering the transformation. I've never known——' he stopped, and she was sure that he had been about to say that he had never known Ishbel to prepare so quickly for an evening out.

'I forgot to mention it when you were in the office yesterday—I have your great-aunt's jewellery in my safe,' he told her as they drove away from the cottage. 'There were a few pieces she wanted close friends to have, but the rest is yours. I'll bring it out to you.'

'I never wear jewellery.'

'She didn't wear it very often, but what she had was good. If you want me to keep it for you in the office I will, but you must have a look at it. It has to be checked and signed for.'

Jessica lost interest, absorbed in the gardens they passed on their way to the Brodie house. Everything was business as far as Adam Brodie was concerned—at least, everything connected with her!

The Brodies lived in a large house about a mile away from Rowan Cottage, beyond the opposite end of the village. It was set in its own large garden and isolated from the other houses by trees. Even in the evening light the front garden was colourful, and as Jessica stepped out of the car the sweet perfume of night-scented stock filled the air.

James Brodie himself opened the door, beaming a welcome. 'My dear Jessica, come in—welcome to my home!'

She stepped into a square hall which had as its centre-piece a round dark table bearing a huge vase of flowers. There was a delicious smell wafting through the house, and the clatter of pots came from the rear of the house. Somewhere, she heard the dogs barking. James led her into the sitting-room and settled her in a large armchair before bringing a glass of sherry to her.

'I had begun to wonder if you had been held up somewhere.'

'We were,' his son said dryly as he took a glass of sherry from James. The older man sat opposite Jessica, but Adam roamed the room restlessly.

'It was my fault. I was working in the garden, and I quite forgot what time it was,' Jessica confessed.

'Now that's what Adam does. Gardens are timeless places.'

'Adam? You mean that you like gardening?' She turned to stare at him, but he shrugged, turning away to study a painting on the wall.

'Adam should have been a gardener,' his father chuckled. 'He looks after this garden. And of course, he tended the garden at Rowan Cottage for the past few years. Hasn't he told you about that?'

Jessica was stunned. It had never occurred to her that Adam Brodie himself had kept the cottage garden so neat. She stared into the depths of her glass, remembering how scathing she had

been earlier—and how remote he had seemed
when he found her gardening. Why couldn't he
unbend and admit to being human?

A smiling housekeeper announced that the
meal was ready and James escorted Jessica into
the dining-room, a panelled room with heavy
velvet curtains drawn against the night. Glasses
and silver on the long oak table glittered in the
light of candles in long, elegant silver candle-
sticks.

'This is beautiful!'

James seated her and took his own seat across
from her. Adam moved to the end of the table,
where he was almost lost in the shadows.

'I'm glad you approve,' James said contentedly
as soup was served from a large tureen. 'We don't
use this room much, of course. This is all in your
honour. Kate—your great-aunt, that is—came
here sometimes, and she and I enjoyed eating
with some dignity. Normally I have a tray by the
fire, or eat in the kitchen.' He poured wine into
Jessica's glass.

'I suppose this is too elaborate for just two of
you,' she agreed, indicating the beautifully
arranged table.

'For just one of us. Adam and I don't live
together—not entirely, that is. He converted the
upper floor into an independent flat when he took
the business over,' his father explained. 'He has a
separate entrance at the side of the house. To all
intents and purposes, you see, we each live alone.'

There was a momentary sadness in his face and
in his voice. Jessica glanced at the other end of

the table but Adam, toying with his glass of wine, merely said, 'It was the most sensible arrangement—under the circumstances.'

'Well, that's of no interest to our guest,' James said briskly, and turned his attention to Jessica. She found herself beginning to like him very much, even on short acquaintance. He had all the qualities his son lacked—charm, warmth, enthusiasm. During the rest of the meal and later, when they had returned to the sitting-room fire with their coffee, she found herself talking freely, amusingly, about her work, her pupils, her parents, and her small flat in Middlesex.

'Don't you get lonely, living alone at your age?'

'Not at all. I've always enjoyed my own company, and I have friends, when I feel the need for company. But after a day in the classroom it's lovely to spend a few hours totally alone, and with silence! That's what appeals to me about Broominch and Rowan Cottage.'

'And you're planning to stay?'

'For the rest of the holiday period. Then I'll decide what to do next.'

Adam, who had been content to let his father and Jessica dominate the conversation, said abruptly, 'But your work is in England.'

'It doesn't have to be. I could move to another school—and I took a secretarial course when I was waiting to go into college. I wasn't sure that teaching was what I wanted to do all my life. I can turn my hand to an office career.'

'An independent young lady.' There was admiration in James's voice. 'Like Kate Ogilvie.

Now I'm beginning to know why she chose to leave her cottage to you.'

'That's more than I know,' Jessica admitted. 'We hardly knew each other, you know. She came South occasionally, and as my parents were abroad I took her on shopping trips and out for meals. But she didn't seem to be interested in me. We never really talked. Why should she leave everything to me?'

'Kate always had her own reasons for doing things. Now that you've decided to spend some time in the cottage, you might grow to know and understand her,' James said softly.

When Jessica reluctantly rose to go at the end of the evening, he took her hand. 'We must meet often while you're here. I hope you'll feel free to come here at any time.'

She smiled up at him. 'I'd love to.'

'If you take Miss Taylor to the car, father, I'll join you in a few minutes,' Adam said stiffly as they went into the hall. He went up a wide staircase at the rear of the hall as James put the white shawl about Jessica's shoulders. Then Adam reappeared, coming round the side of the house as Jessica got into the car. A Labrador was by his side, and when he opened the driver's door and pulled the seat forward, the big dog obediently jumped into the back seat and settled down.

'I thought you could do with company, since you're going to stay alone at the cottage,' Adam explained as he got into the car. Jessica sat upright.

'What? If you think I want to get knocked down every time I move in my own house, you're——'

'This,' he said in the patient, explaining-it-to-an-idiot voice he tended to use for her benefit, 'is Cleopatra. Cleo for short. She's Toby's mother, and extremely obedient.'

The dog whined softly as she heard her name mentioned. Adam started the car, and as it turned out of the gate Jessica turned to wave. James Brodie seemed a solitary figure, outlined against the lighted doorway of his house, and she wondered about the lack of warmth between him and his son. It all seemed to be on Adam's side.

'I'll be quite all right in the cottage, you know,' she protested as the car headed through the village. 'You surely don't expect me to be inundated with burglars or vandals, do you?'

'Not in this part of the world.'

'And I'm used to living on my own, you know that.'

He glanced at her, then back at the road. She wasn't to know how young, how small and vulnerable she looked to him. 'You usually live in a flat, with people on the other side of the wall.'

'Great-aunt Kate didn't have a dog, did she?'

'As a matter of fact, she did. A very old Pekinese who had to be put down when Miss Ogilvie died, I'm afraid.'

'Not exactly a watch-dog.'

He didn't take his eyes from the road. 'You haven't lived in a fairly remote cottage by yourself. And you're my client. I feel responsible in a way for your welfare.'

'I wish,' said Jessica in exasperation, 'that you would treat me like a client, and not like an irresponsible child!'

'Do I?' Just for a moment she thought a look of amusement crossed his face, but it was gone before she could be certain.

'According to you I'm not fit to own a cottage, or to decide what should be done with it, or to live there alone—you're a bully, Mr Brodie!'

He pulled the car into the open space by the cottage gate, cut the engine and turned to her, a dark outline against the night outside. 'No, I'm just a lawyer who's good at his job.'

'And I'm good at mine, so why——'

'So you keep telling me.' He leaned across her and opened the passenger door. Soft, thick hair brushed against her cheek, bringing with it that scent of the outdoors. Then he was opening his own door.

'Come on, Cleo. I'll settle her before I go home.'

The dog trotted off to examine the verge and Adam Brodie opened the boot of his car. Jessica unlocked the cottage door. It was the first time she had been in the house at night, and the sitting-room looked cosy in the light from two lamps, one on either side of the fire. Cleo padded in a few minutes later, and Jessica knelt to stroke her.

'It looks as though we're going to be seeing a lot of each other,' she told the dog. 'So we might as well get acquainted. And I hope you don't snore.'

Cleo sniffed delicately at the fingers Jessica held out, then licked them. As Jessica ran her hand again over the dog's glossy coat, Adam Brodie appeared in the doorway, a box and a heavy blanket in his arms.

'Looks as though she's taken to you.'

'I like dogs.'

He put the box and blanket down. 'I'll make up a fire, if you like. It gets cool in the evenings.' Moving as though he was at home in the place, he found an old newspaper beneath a chair cushion, crumpled it up, and took wood from the log box by the fireplace.

'Miss Ogilvie kept this box well filled—she loved a log fire. The Stevensons up at the stables provided her with wood. There's still plenty of it in that shed by the side of the house.'

She looked down at his bent head as he deftly arranged the wood and then took matches from his pocket.

'Would you—would you like some coffee?' she offered tentatively.

He looked up and smiled at her, a smile that transformed his serious face and lapped round Jessica with a warmth that almost took her breath away.

'Actually,' he said, 'I was beginning to think you'd never offer.'

CHAPTER THREE

IT was silly to be so happy just because a moody man had finally summoned up a smile, Jessica told herself. But she glowed as she drew flowered curtains across the sitting-room windows and went into the kitchen to fill the kettle.

The sudden crack in Adam Brodie's armour made her feel for the first time that he could be a friend, rather than an enemy.

'It's the teacher in you!' she told herself, setting out bright-coloured mugs and measuring coffee into them. Indeed, there had been times when she felt that glow—when a difficult child in school had finally responded to her.

Flames licked strongly round the logs in the fireplace when she carried the mugs into the next room. Adam Brodie was stretched out in an armchair, long legs sprawled across the rug. Cleo was curled up on the rug, her muzzle on his foot. He looked quite at home.

'Did you visit my aunt here often?'

'Quite a lot. Over the past two years, since I took charge of the office, she wasn't able to get out and about at times. I came here when we had to do business, and I drove her over to have dinner with my father now and then.'

'And you looked after her garden.' She waited,

47

but he said nothing. 'You haven't always lived in Broominch, have you?'

He raised his eyebrows. 'What's this—the third degree?'

'You heard all about me tonight—now I'll admit to being curious about you,' she dared to say.

'I must apologise for my father. Older people sometimes seem to think that they have the right to be inquisitive.'

'He wasn't inquisitive, he was interested in me.'

'And you like that?'

'I like people who care about other people. Don't you?'

There was a pause, then, 'Not particularly. But since you ask—I was born and brought up here, then I worked in England for several years. I came back two years ago after my father had suffered a serious heart attack, and took over the office.'

'For his sake.'

'No—because I thought it was my duty.'

'But why would you——?'

'The very old—and the very young—are inquisitive,' Adam Brodie cut in, and Jessica flushed.

'There you go again—treating me as though I was a child!'

'You look like one, sitting on the rug beside Cleo.'

She scrambled to her feet, and the dog lifted her head for a moment before settling herself again, with a sigh. 'I can't help it if I don't look my age! It's a family failing.'

'Miss Ogilvie certainly didn't look her age,' he admitted.

'You were fond of her, weren't you?'

'She was—a fine person. We enjoyed each other's company, and I felt that I could trust her.'

'Don't you usually trust people?'

His mouth hardened and his eyes were wary. 'I learned long ago that trusting people leads to being hurt.'

'Getting hurt now and then is part of being alive.' Jessica took the empty mug from his hand and put it on the table. 'I take it that your mother——'

'Is dead,' he finished the sentence and rose in one swift movement. 'I've taken up enough of your time. Thank you for the coffee.' He picked up the blanket and the box which, she now saw, held tins of dog food. 'I'll put this in the kitchen. Cleo can sleep there. She gets fed morning and night, and don't overdo it or she'll get fat.'

He put the blanket and box in the kitchen, came back to the sitting-room and squatted down to take the dog's head in both hands. 'Stay here, girl—hear me? That's a good girl.'

Jessica watched man and dog, noting the gentleness in Adam's touch, the warmth in his voice. 'You could take her back home, really. I'll be quite all right by myself,' she said, suddenly impatient. She wanted no favours from anyone, least of all this bewildering man. He looked up at her.

'You're my client. I'm responsible for your safety. If you insist on staying here by yourself, I have to make sure that you're all right.'

'But you don't have to like doing your duty, do you? You're old-fashioned, Mr Brodie. Duty doesn't have to be something carried out in bitterness. And you aren't going to make me feel grateful to you for your help. Women got the vote some time ago, though nobody appears to have told you about it. We can look after ourselves.'

She turned towards the door as she spoke, intent on showing him out before her temper broke. But as she put her fingers on the handle her arm was caught in a strong grip, and before she had time to do more than utter a squeak of protest she found herself whirled round and into his arms.

'What are——? Let me go at once!' She struggled, but he held her with no effort at all.

'I'm showing you that you can't always take care of yourself,' he said into her hair. 'What would you do if I was a stranger, an intruder?'

She lashed out viciously with one foot, then yelped as her stockinged toes connected with his leg and a wave of pain shot through her foot. Adam loosened his grip, then had to catch her in his arms again as she collapsed against him.

'A fine idea—if you're prepared to wear clogs all the time.'

'First your dog ladders my stockings, and then you break my toes!' she stormed against his shoulder. 'Why can't you just leave me alone?'

She glared up at him, then stopped struggling as she saw the wondering look in the brown eyes close to her own. 'I wish I could——' Adam said, his voice husky and uncertain, then he bent his head and kissed her; gently at first, then more urgently as her lips parted slightly beneath his. When he released her they stared at each other, dazed. Jessica moved back a step, shakily.

'Do you always treat female clients like this?' she asked breathlessly.

He blinked, then turned away, running one hand through his hair. 'I'm sorry, I had no right to do that. It was just——' He headed for the door. 'I'd better go.'

'Adam——' She didn't realise until later that she had used his first name. His face was expressionless as he turned back into the room.

'I told you, you shouldn't trust anyone—even your lawyer,' he said bleakly, and opened the door. By the time she reached the hall he was outside on the path, a dark silhouette against the summer night's sky. 'Are you all right?'

'All right?'

'Your foot.'

'Oh——' Jessica had forgotten about her bruised toes. 'Yes, I'm fine.'

He hesitated, and she thought, hoped, that he was about to say something. Then he nodded and turned away. Jessica closed the door and stood in the hall, listening as the car door slammed, the engine started up, and then dwindled into the distance.

The cottage seemed empty without him, and

she was glad of Cleo's company as she washed the mugs and made more coffee. She sat for a long time in the chair Adam had occupied, staring into the hearth. The fire he had kindled had almost burned itself out before Jessica went to bed, leaving Cleo in the kitchen.

She lay in bed watching the moon through the window, listening to the night sounds, puzzling over Adam's abrupt departure, remembering his arms about her, his lips on hers.

She wasn't naïve—and she wasn't an idiot either, she told the moon firmly. She knew that his kiss had been on impulse, something that had just happened before either of them realised it. An enjoyable kiss—and totally unexpected from someone as withdrawn as Adam. She knew that it meant nothing—but she was concerned over his refusal to stay. If it meant that he thought she was the type to get all excited and flustered over one kiss, he was a fool. And, she realised wryly, it would complicate matters again, just when he had begun to unbend a little.

She turned over, made a firm resolution to behave, when she met him again, as though the kiss had never happened, and fell asleep.

Cleo wakened her in the morning, padding upstairs and through the open bedroom door to lay her muzzle on the bed, whining softly. Jessica woke with a start and found the dog eyeing her hopefully. Yawning, she went downstairs and let Cleo out of the back door, following her into the garden, luxuriating in the cool, dew-damp grass beneath her bare feet. It was a beautiful morning—too beautiful to waste. Leaving Cleo to explore the garden, Jessica hurried upstairs and slipped into a russet-coloured sweater and black trousers. She put on sturdy shoes and she and Cleo set off for a walk.

She hesitated at the foot of the lane to the Stevenson farm, where Ishbel lived. There was a notice board she had not seen before, reading 'Broominch Farm Riding Stables. A. Stevenson.' A bend at the far end of the tree-lined lane hid the house from view, allowing only a glimpse of white walls through the greenery. Jessica followed a path farther along the road, and Cleo trotted obediently by her side, apparently quite content with her temporary owner.

'I wish your son was as obedient as you are,' Jessica told her, and the dog licked her hand, then ran ahead as the path opened out into a field sloping up to a belt of trees.

After the routine of school life it was heavenly to have the whole day to herself, with nobody making claims on her time. Jessica happily explored thickets, little narrow valleys with burns chattering through them, and hillsides thick with high ferns, before hunger made her look at her watch. She had been away from the cottage for two hours, and hadn't had anything to eat.

'And neither have you—poor old Cleo, what a rotten hostess I am! Come on, time to go home.' She turned and looked down the hill she stood on. Broominch could be seen below, a cluster of houses among trees, with the road glimpsed here and there. She was able to pick out the stables, and followed the double line of trees lining the lane until she saw the chimneys of Rowan Cottage, almost buried in greenery. She must have walked in a curve, but it looked as though she could go back in a straight line from where she stood.

The hill led into a small area of woodland, the ground beneath the trees soft and springy, and then into a paddock with brightly-coloured stands and bars set up for jumping. As Jessica emerged from beneath the shelter of the trees she saw that a large black horse was being put over the jumps. She called Cleo to her and turned to skirt the paddock, but the rider called to her, turning the horse away from the jumps and walking it over to Jessica.

'Good morning!' It was Ishbel Stevenson, trim in a thick sweater and jodhpurs, her black hair hidden beneath a hard hat. 'Having a look around?'

Jessica stroked the animal's soft nose. 'Am I trespassing?'

'Good heavens, no—you're welcome to go anywhere you like on our land. After all,' said Ishbel sweetly, 'you're living on it, for the time being. Isn't that Cleo?' she nodded to where the dog was exploring the roots of a large old tree.

'Adam—Mr Brodie—thought I needed protection while I was in Rowan Cottage.'

Ishbel raised her eyebrows. 'Really? You'll have to come to the house some time, Jessica. I'd invite you to lunch, but we have a full day today—always plenty of pupils during the

holidays. Come this evening, for a drink. My
mother would like to meet you, and my brother's
at home just now.'

Jessica felt that she had no choice but to accept
the invitation, though she would have preferred
the entire day to herself.

'About eight o'clock then?' Ishbel slapped the
horse's neck lightly with the reins. 'Now I have
to finish his workout and collect a party of
beginners. See you later.'

Jessica stayed and watched for a few minutes,
envying the other girl's superb horsemanship as
she took the big horse over jump after jump.
Then she remembered that she and Cleo hadn't
eaten, and headed again for home.

Finding the cottage empty and Jessica's car
parked by the gate, Adam waited on the front
steps in the sun. Eventually Toby became
restless, and Adam walked him along the road
and along the path to the fields. He looked up the
hill, and saw Cleo and Jessica emerging from the
trees some distance away. With a yelp of delight
Toby rushed up the hill towards Cleo, who
almost bowled him over in her haste to reach
Adam.

'Hello, girl—been behaving yourself, have
you?' He hugged the dog, then sat on a fallen tree
and waited for Jessica. Her russet sweater was a
patch of glowing colour against the green of the
hill, and her hair was caught by a breeze and
whisked across her face as he watched. She
looked, he thought again, like a child. For the
twentieth time he remembered the softness of her

lips against his, the warmth of her in his arms, and cursed himself for being a clumsy, stupid oaf. He had enough to cope with without this girl who had intruded into his life. The sooner she was back in England, the better, Adam thought darkly.

Jessica could tell by the firm lips and distant eyes that he was regretting that moment in the cottage. She took a deep breath, lifted her chin in unconscious defiance, and smiled. 'Good morning, Mr Brodie.'

'Toby!' Adam's voice was like the crack of a whip, and the young dog checked his enthusiastic rush towards Jessica, contenting himself with licking her hand. She knelt on the grass to stroke him.

'I called to give Cleo a walk.'

'We decided on that hours ago, didn't we, Cleo? I'm quite capable of looking after her, you know.'

'I would hardly have left her with you if I hadn't trusted you, Miss Taylor.'

'Look, I know you're my lawyer and I'm your client, but couldn't we be on first-name terms?'

'I don't think that——'

She interrupted him, colour rising into her face. 'I know what's wrong—you're embarrassed about what happened last night. Please don't be. I've forgotten it—well, I couldn't have forgotten it or I wouldn't be able to mention it, would I? What I mean is——' she rushed on, not daring to meet his eyes, 'I think we should both forget it. It was a misunderstanding.'

'I owe you an apology.'

'No, you dont! It was as much my fault as it was yours. I mean—can't we just forget it ever happened? And can't you treat me like a person, not a client? "Miss Taylor" makes me feel like a schoolmarm, and you're rather large to be one of my pupils. They're only about seven years old, you see.'

Now she dared to look up at his face, and saw that he was amused. 'Well, as I can't imagine you as a schoolteacher, I suppose I'll have to stop calling you "Miss".'

'And another request. Could we stop this ridiculous conversation and go and eat? Cleo and I are starving!'

Back in the cottage she went upstairs to brush her wind-tossed hair, change out of her sturdy shoes, and put on a cool blue-and-white checked shirt in place of the russet sweater. She went back into the kitchen to find Adam whipping eggs into pale gold froth in a bowl.

'Scrambled eggs be all right? Don't look so surprised, I'm used to doing my own cooking. And I've put in enough for two.'

They ate picnic-fashion in the back garden while the dogs lolled in the shade of the willow tree. Prompted by Jessica, Adam talked a little about the village and his childhood there.

'Didn't you miss it while you were in England?'

He shook his dark head. 'Not particularly. Things change, and I was quite glad to get out of the place.'

'And yet you came back.'

He glanced quickly at her, then away again. 'I told you, it was my duty.' And he changed the subject.

He left soon afterwards, taking Toby with him, and Jessica devoted the rest of the afternoon to lazing in the garden with one of Great-aunt Kate's books. On the flyleaf she found an inscription 'To Kate, from Edward,' with a date in the nineteen-thirties. Sleepy in the heat of the sun, lulled by the drone of bees among the fronds of the lilacs, Jessica pondered over the names. Kate and Edward. A love affair? She thought of Kate Ogilvie as she had known her, a tall, thin, elegant old lady with immaculate white hair and a somewhat severe expression, and tried to picture her as a young woman, loved by the unknown Edward.

Until the day it had been announced that the cottage had been left to Jessica, she'd known nothing of Kate. As far as the family was concerned, she was an elderly relative, living quite far away. A woman without a past—or perhaps, Jessica mused drowsily, running one finger over the inscription, a woman who kept her secrets well. She turned over on to her stomach on the grass, and gazed at the back of the cottage, at its twinkling windows with their neat curtains, at the sturdy walls and bright flower-beds filled to overflowing with pansies, lupins, poppies and snapdragons. Anyone who had lived here for years, who had loved and cherished the place as Kate had done, must be a special person.

And she determined to find out more about Kate Ogilvie.

After eating her evening meal, Jessica looked through the drawers of the little writing-bureau in the sitting-room. There were no letters, no photographs, only a neat stack of notepaper, a packet of envelopes, pens and pencils, blotting-paper. Jessica closed the bureau with a sense of disappointment, and went upstairs to get ready for her visit to the Stevensons.

She took Cleo for a short walk, then left her in the cottage and made her way up the lane towards the Stevenson house. As she turned the bend at the top of the lane she stopped to take in the house before her. It had once been a solid, matter-of-fact farmhouse, but now the large courtyard was spotlessly clean, the old flagstones levelled and swept to reveal their soft grey shades, a contrast to the huge containers filled with multi-coloured flowers that stood here and there. The house itself was of light grey stone with white woodwork and a large, sturdy wooden door flanked by enormous painted cart wheels. To one side, a wrought-iron gate in a high wall revealed a glimpse of smooth green lawn and flower beds at the side of the house. A sign on the opposite corner of the building indicated the way to the stables and riding school offices.

She blinked as the door opened, for the man standing there was one of the handsomest men she had seen in a long time. His hair was black, and his eyes were a deep, dark-lashed blue. When he grinned, white teeth emphasised his smooth even tan.

'You've got to be Jessica—right?' He drew her into the hall. 'I'm David—Ishbel's brother. And——' his eyes swept over her with open approval, 'I'm delighted to meet you. They're all out on the terrace. I'll take your jacket, it's warm out there. The old stones hold the heat after the sun goes down.' He slipped the jacket from around her shoulders as he talked, took her elbow in a friendly grasp, and steered her through a large, comfortable sitting-room and out of the open French windows on to the terrace.

'Here she is.'

'Jessica!' Ishbel, beautiful in white tailored slacks and a gold-coloured shirt trimmed with bronze, rose easily from a garden chair. 'Come and meet everyone. You know David—this is my mother—and this is——'

'We already know each other,' James Brodie said, getting to his feet. 'And I'm delighted to see you again, Jessica. Come and sit over here. The privilege of being an older man,' he added to David, who had been about to steer Jessica to a double seat. 'Annette sometimes takes pity on me, and invites me over for a meal,' he explained to Jessica. 'I never refuse, because she's an excellent cook.'

'When I get the time, which isn't often. And I don't have to be an excellent cook to provide the salad I served tonight, James,' Ishbel's mother said dryly. She was a tall, angular woman with short grey hair and a face that looked aloof when serious, but warm and friendly when she smiled.

She was nut-brown, with the strong tanned skin of someone who was outdoors most of the year, and wore her long, loose dull-orange dress with a slightly uncomfortable air. Jessica realised, as she listened to the conversation, that Mrs Stevenson was only happy when she was wearing casual outdoor clothes, and working with her beloved horses. She bore no resemblance to her black-haired, blue-eyed son and daughter, and Jessica supposed that they took their stunning looks from their father.

'We should have invited you to the house for dinner—I would have, if I'd know that you and James were friends,' Mrs Stevenson explained to Jessica. 'But—well——'

'Horses come first in this household,' David cut in teasingly. 'We eat when we're hungry, and we can never be sure that we'll all sit at the table together. We daren't invite strangers for a meal until we've warned them.'

'Do you work with horses, too?'

Ishbel's scoffing laughter was ignored by her brother. 'No, thank you! They threw me out when I was eighteen—made me go to college. They allow me to spend the holidays here; I'm between Finals and a new job in Edinburgh now.'

'Actually, he's very brainy,' Ishbel told Jessica. 'Too brainy for this place. He's an accountant. And he can't ride well.'

'A glorified pen-pusher,' David lamented. 'All that training because those two——' he jerked his head towards his mother and sister, 'want free financial advice. Er—you did ask the girl here for a drink, didn't you, Ishbel? What would you like, Jessica?'

Looking at the immaculate garden, aware of the bulk of the old house behind her, Jessica guessed that Mrs Stevenson must have a fairly good head for finance herself. It was clear that the stables paid well. She accepted a drink from David and listened while the family and James Brodie talked about the riding school. Mrs Stevenson was calling on James to agree with her that Ishbel should take up the offer of a course in an English riding centre, but the girl was reluctant.

'You're mad if you turn it down,' her mother told her. 'You may not get in easily next year, and it would make all the difference to us if you had added qualifications. Besides, you were very keen last year to try the course.'

'I know, but—well, I don't particularly want to go away just now,' her daughter protested, her lovely face petulant.

'Aha!' David pounced. 'Got a special reason, sister?'

'Oh, shut up!' she snapped, and flounced down the steps to the garden, where she pulled at the leaves of a rosebush. Then her dark head lifted eagerly as a car was heard coming up the lane.

'Here comes the reason,' David murmured, and his mother frowned at him.

'Don't tease her, David! Honestly, life is so quiet when those two are living in separate places!' she confided to Jessica, who was uncomfortably reminded of Ishbel's intention to buy Rowan Cottage so that she would have somewhere private, where she could be on her own.

'Adam!' Ishbel ran to the iron gate in the wall and opened it as Adam Brodie's tall figure appeared. She stood on tiptoe and kissed him lightly, then linked her hand in his arm as they came to the terrace. Glancing at James Brodie, Jessica saw a very faint frown as he watched his son and Ishbel.

Adam raised his brows slightly when he saw Jessica, but he only said mildly, 'I didn't realise you'd be here, Miss Taylor.'

'Jessica!' Ishbel told him firmly. 'She's more or less one of the family now, aren't you, Jessica? Same as usual, Adam?' She waved David back to his chair and began to pour out a drink for Adam, who sat down on the terrace steps, leaning against the stone wall that flanked them. Ishbel handed him the glass then sat beside him. 'You look as though you've had a hard day at the office.' She touched the serious lines at one corner of his mouth with the tip of a finger. 'Smile, you're among friends now.'

He smiled slightly, and sipped at his drink. 'Hard enough.' His hair, Jessica noticed, was allowed to go its own way when he wasn't dressed for the office. There was the suggestion of a wave in it, and it framed his face with soft springy tendrils. He suited it that way, she thought. Suddenly his clear brown eyes flicked up to her face, a mild question in their depths, and she flushed, realising that she had been staring.

Embarrassed, she turned to David, asking him about his new job.

'Oh, don't let's talk about that,' he said easily, smiling deep into her eyes. 'I let things happen in their own good time. A good philosophy, don't you think?'

'I wouldn't know. I've always had to think ahead.'

David's gaze held her, sent a slow tingle coursing through her. 'That way lies danger, my love—didn't they ever tell you that? Much better to let life carry you along. Look at Adam there. He's too serious, and where has it got him?'

'Further than you'll get if you don't change your attitude,' Adam's deep voice told him placidly.

David turned to grin at him. 'I don't know about that. You don't seem to have any fun out of life, as far as I can tell. And you're getting on a bit, aren't you? How many years now? Thirty-five?'

'Thirty-three—still young enough to beat the living daylights out of you on the tennis court,' Adam said, still unruffled. Mrs Stevenson smiled as she watched the two of them, and Jessica realised that this was a normal conversation between the men. Adam treated David as though he was a kid brother, and it was obvious, watching him among the Stevenson family, that he spent a lot of time with them.

She felt an unaccustomed stab of pain. Could it be jealousy? She had never felt the need for a large family of brothers or sisters, had never felt homesick for her parents when they moved to Spain. But she put the twinge of jealousy down to the way Adam, an only child himself, had found a family. And she guessed, looking at the slim hand Ishbel placed possessively on Adam's arm, that one day he would be absorbed completely into this little circle.

Clearly, that was Ishbel's intention, though Adam himself had neither said nor done anything to indicate that he was going along with her plans, Jessica realised. But on the other hand, he hadn't shown any resistance. And, as Ishbel said herself, she always got her own way in the end.

CHAPTER FOUR

'Has Ishbel said anything to you about Rowan Cottage?' David asked as he and Jessica strolled across the lawn in the dusk. Behind them the house was shimmering against the darkening sky, a pale ghost of its daytime self. James Brodie and Annette Stevenson had gone off to visit friends, and Jessica had been invited to stay a little longer.

'If you mean do I know she wants it—she told me as soon as we met.'

'And?'

They were passing the flower beds that edged the grass. Clusters of Canterbury bells seemed to hang motionless in mid-air, their slender stalks invisible, the misty blue globes almost glowing in the dim light.

'Are you a counter-spy?' Jessica asked with interest. 'Have you been told to persuade me to sell to your sister?'

He threw back his head and laughed aloud. 'I like you, Jessica Taylor, you're very straight-forward. No, I'm not trying to persuade you, though yes, Ishbel would like us all to work at it. I don't need to lobby on her behalf, she always gets what she wants. She was a horror when we were young—Dad encouraged her all the way, and never denied her anything.' There was no resentment in his voice, only amusement. 'She thinks that if she gets Rowan Cottage she'll be independent—playing at dolls' houses, if you ask me.'

It was Jessica's turn to laugh. 'That's what I'm doing, I suppose. It is like a doll's house!'

'Yes, but you're used to living your own life, aren't you? Ishbel wants to have her cake and eat it. Stay with the stables, and Broominch, and yet be independent. It won't work. She can't stay at home, and be independent, even in the cottage.'

'Your mother doesn't strike me as the dominating type—surely she wouldn't want to keep Ishbel at home indefinitely.'

'Not a bit of it. All she wants are the stables, and her horses. She sold off most of the farmland for building after Dad died, and put the money into the stables. She's not the maternal sort—unless you've got four hooves, that is. No, Dad spoiled Ishbel, and she still feels safer when she's near home. That's why she's kicking at the thought of going on this course, though it's just what she needs.'

'And—there's Adam,' Jessica said deliberately, turning to look back at the two figures sitting on the terrace steps.

'There's Adam—in a way. Ishbel wants to get him to the altar, poor man. She used to worship him when we were kids and he was the big schoolboy who knew everything in the world. And when he came back to Broominch she more or less claimed him for her own. But I reckon she's hooked a fish that doesn't want to get caught.'

'A woman-hater?'

David shrugged. 'I don't think so. Just not in favour of marriage—and with a touch of insanity, of course. A lovely girl like you comes along, straight into his office, and I bet he hasn't even made a pass at you yet, has he?'

All at once she remembered that moment in Adam's arms, the warm, sure touch of his mouth on hers, the bewilderment in his eyes as he drew back to stare down at her. And all at once she was glad that the night hid the colour that rushed into her face.

'Of course not! For goodness' sake, I'm a client, as you say, and nothing more!'

Without realising it, she had quickened her step, and David had to hurry to catch up with her. 'No need to get into a tizzy about it,' he protested, laughing. 'All I was going to say was that if someone like you walked into my office I'd take more than a passing interest.'

'Perhaps it's as well you're not a lawyer, then, or you'd find yourself getting into one mess after another.'

'I have hopes that even an accountant might meet an occasional beautiful woman,' he assured her. 'Talking of beauty, have you realised that your dress is the same colour as those Canterbury bells behind you? In fact, I don't know why we're wasting time talking about Ishbel and Adam when we would talk about you and me. Come out with me tomorrow.'

The suggestion was sudden, and her reaction

was equally sudden. 'No, thank you.'

'Why not? Don't you fancy me?'

She looked up at him, outlined against the sky, his teeth gleaming in an infectious grin. He was very good-looking, and she felt a thrill of pleasure at his flattering interest. But life had picked her up and rushed her along too quickly since her arrival in Broominch, and she needed a respite.

'I just want to have a little time to myself, to catch up and get to know the cottage,' she said truthfully, and David sighed, steering her back to the terrace with one arm carelessly draped round her shoulders.

'It's not often that I'm rejected—but I shall try again,' he warned her, and she found herself hoping that he would. By the time they got back to the terrace he had had another thought. 'Ishbel, what about that hop you wanted me to go to?'

'The Young Farmer's annual dance is not a hop, David, it is a local occasion. And it's on Friday.'

'That's the one. Well—why not make it a foursome? You two, and me and Jessica.'

Ishbel raised an eyebrow. 'You said that you wouldn't be caught dead at the dance, remember?'

'Ah—that was because I hadn't met Jessica. What about it, Jessica—will you let me escort you to the ball? Pumpkins at midnight and all that sort of thing?'

'But I've got nothing to wear——'

'David, I don't think Jessica wants to be

bothered with local dances.' Adam's voice was irritable, and suddenly Jessica felt a spark of resentment.

'—but I can buy something before Friday,' she finished the sentence smoothly, without looking at Adam. 'Thank you, David, I'd love to come to the dance with you.'

When she got up to go a little later Adam announced that he, too, was leaving. Ishbel pouted, but her efforts to get him to stay on were ignored.

His car was waiting in the courtyard, and Jessica shook her head as he opened the passenger door. 'It's not worth getting into a car for that short drive down the lane. I'd rather walk.'

'Nevertheless——' his hand closed over her arm, and before she realised what was happening, she had been whisked into the car and Adam was walking round to the driver's door.

'Do you usually press-gang people like that?' The car was on its way down the drive before she recovered the use of her voice.

'I wanted to talk to you.'

'And that gives you the right to treat me like a naughty little girl?' she snapped.

He turned and eyed her as the car came to a standstill by her gate. 'I'd hardly describe you as "naughty". May I come in for a moment?'

'I'd rather you didn't,' she said bluntly, and saw his eyes widen in the dim light, a smile beginning to tug at the corners of his well-shaped mouth. 'I've told you before, Mr Brodie—

Adam—that I am not a child. You do not have to order me about. And I know you don't want me to go to that dance, but——'

His hand moved and the interior light clicked on. 'I don't object to your going to the dance.'

'But you were annoyed when I accepted—I could tell!'

She could have kicked him when he answered, 'One up for women's intuition—even though it's wrong this time.'

'Are you trying to tell me now that you don't object to having to put up with my company on Friday evening?'

'My dear girl,' said Adam Brodie, 'you can go to every disco and gig from here to Edinburgh, if it gives you pleasure. I only want to warn you against getting too involved with David Stevenson. He's—well, he's a good-looking boy, but he knows it. He looks on women as a challenge, and I just don't think you should put too much trust in him, that's all.'

Jessica banged on the dash with both fists. 'Adam, you are not my keeper, my father, my agony aunt—and you're talking like an elderly stuffed shirt!'

He twisted in his seat to look at her, the even, reasonable voice suddenly thick with anger. 'I'm what? Now look here——'

'You're jealous!' she accused. 'Jealous because he's younger than you are, and more fun, and—and he's got a much more exciting life-style!'

'And what do you know about——' he began, but she rushed on.

'Anyway, he's Ishbel's brother—you shouldn't be running down someone's who's probably going to be an in-law!'

He caught at her wrists, turned her to face him. Anger and astonishment played over his strong features, 'What the hell does that mean?' he almost shouted at her.

'You and Ishbel—obviously you'll marry one day——'

'Obviously? Is that what you think—or is that what you've been told?'

'It's there for anyone to see, for heaven's sake. I'm not blind!' The words trailed off as he released her wrists, and opened the car door.

'I'll give Cleo a run before I go home,' he said coolly, formally, as she got out of the car.

'I'll do it.' She was unable to make out his expression as he loomed above her. 'Cleo is meant to be a guard dog. She'll guard me while I'm exercising her. Goodnight, Adam. And thank you for the lift home.'

He was still by the car, watching her, as she slipped into the cottage. Cleo welcomed her with enthusiasm, and she shut the door quickly, not wanting the dog to sense Adam's presence outside.

His car door slammed as soon as she was in the hall, and the car drove off. Jessica changed into a warm sweater and jeans, thinking, as she hung up the misty blue dress, of David's words, 'Talking of beauty, have you realised that your dress is the same colour as the Canterbury bells?' It was one of her favourite dresses, and her spirits rose as she stroked the soft material into place. It was lovely to meet someone as amusing, as handsome, as openly interested as David Stevenson. He could well make her stay in Broominch something special. If only Adam hadn't tried to intervene with his malicious remarks—Jessica frowned as she collected the dog and took her to the field behind Rowan Cottage. She would make up her own mind about David, and she would refuse to let Adam Brodie domineer her any longer. After all, she wasn't looking for marriage from David, just a pleasant, relaxed companion.

She wondered, briefly, about Adam's anger when she referred to marriage between himself and Ishbel, then decided that Adam was afraid of marriage, afraid of forming a lasting relationship. Strange, too, that he was so unlike his warm, charming father. In fact, Adam Brodie was unlike anyone Jessica had ever met. Annoying, maddening at times—but intriguing, though she felt that it was time she stopped trying to fathom him out, and left him to his own devices, whatever they might be.

She realised on the following morning that if she was to shake loose of Adam's domination, she must return Cleo. She could hardly reject the man's attitude while she allowed his dog to 'protect' her, and there was no reason why she shouldn't stay on her own, anyway. It was a sad decision, because she had become fond of Cleo. She fed the dog, then took her for one last walk before going to the big house at the other end of the village. Somehow, she couldn't face the thought of telling Adam face to face that she was not going to keep Cleo, so she took the coward's way out and called during office hours, when she was sure that he would be out of the way.

The housekeeper beamed as she opened the door. Cleo hurried straight into the hall, pausing to run her warm tongue over the woman's hand in greeting. 'Well—Miss Taylor! Come away in, Mr Brodie's sitting in the garden.'

'I—I thought he'd be at his office!' Jessica's heart flipped uncomfortably. The woman laughed.

'I'm talking about Mr James—I was just going to take his lunch out on a tray, and he'll be pleased to have your company. You must be ready to eat.' Her eyes took in the outdoor clothes, the untidy hair tangled by bushes and overhanging branches.

Aware that she must look a mess, Jessica tried to excuse herself and get back to the cottage, but the women swept her through a large kitchen and out into the garden, where James Brodie sat in the sun. Cleo rushed ahead of them, bowling Toby over when he ran to meet her.

'Jessica, my dear, this is a lovely surprise!' James fussed round, fetching another deck-chair, pouring golden orange-juice from a pitcher which stood in the shade. The housekeeper brought out salad and coffee, and the dogs were ordered to the far end of the garden so that the meal could be eaten in peace.

'I hope that this is a social visit, and not a duty call.'

'I've brought Cleo back,' she confessed, and he raised his eyebrows. 'Has she been a nuisance?'

'No, it's just that—well, I——'

'You don't want a nursemaid,' he suggested, a twinkle in his eyes. Jessica laughed, and found herself explaining quite easily to Adam's father that she resented his son's officious treatment.

'I ask you—do I look helpless?'

James surveyed her thoughtfully. 'I'd say you're a lassie who can think for herself. And Broominch is a quiet place, no need for you to have the dog around if you don't want her. Perhaps Adam's taking his duties too seriously, but he was fond of Kate—we all were——' he added, almost to himself, his eyes sad. 'Adam means well enough.'

'I know that. I just wish he'd let me think things out for myself. He must have been a serious little boy!' she added without stopping to think.

James shifted slightly in his chair, looked up beyond the trees to the clear sky. 'He was a happy wee boy, though you might not think it to see the man he's grown into. I blame myself for what Adam's become.'

Jessica was embarrassed by the pain in the old man's eyes as they met hers. 'I'm sorry, I shouldn't pry into your life.'

But James put up a hand to stop her. 'You didn't pry, my dear. Perhaps you've just made me think back to when I was Adam's age. You see—Adam's mother left Broominch when he was twelve years old. She went away with someone else. And from that day, Adam's blamed me. He was right, too.'

He stopped, and Jessica waited.

'She'd never have looked at anyone else if I'd been a faithful husband,' James said at last. 'I was headstrong in those days, Jessica. I enjoyed life, I enjoyed the company of other women, though the only woman who mattered to me was my own wife. But I never stopped to think that until it was too late. So Adam became bitter towards me, and towards his mother, because she couldn't take him with her. She left him behind, and as soon as he could, he went away too. I don't blame him.'

'But he came back.'

James smiled and shook his head. 'Only because his conscience told him to, when I was very ill. It's a terrible thing, a Scottish Presbyterian conscience, Jessica. It nags at you until you have to do its bidding. We made a bargain, me and Adam. He would run the business, and we would live independent lives in a divided house. Sometimes, though, I wonder if I was right to ask him to come back, for Broominch has unhappy memories for him. He can never forget he's a Brodie, while he's here.'

'What difference does that make?'

He smiled, this time with amusement. 'Women, Jessica! I wasn't the first Brodie to look outside his own door. The Brodies were among the most active of the Border raiders in the old days—but it was rarely cattle they brought back from their forays. They were wild men, right enough!'

A sudden thrill ran through Jessica. Without understanding why, she remembered Adam's grip on her arm as he pushed her into his car at the farm, the undercurrent of strength she had sensed when she fell into his arms in the hall at Rowan Cottage, on their first meeting. Adam Brodie—Then she came back to the present. 'It sounds exciting.'

'I suppose it does, at that. But it's all in the past. And it's no joke for Adam. He's avoided marriage, because of his mother and me. It's a pity, for he's a fine man, and I'd not like him to deny himself happiness because of me.'

Jessica picked a daisy, twirling it between her fingers. 'I thought he disliked women.'

'Adam? Not at all, he's suspicious. He's good-looking—like me, at his age,' James allowed himself a little complacency, 'and he could have married before if he'd had a mind to. He puts up a defence against anyone who might want to interfere in his carefully controlled life. He was fond of Kate Ogilvie, though. She was gentle, understanding—they talked for hours on end at Rowan Cottage you know, when he tended the garden for her. I think that's why he feels responsible for the cottage, and for your welfare.'

Jessica had plenty to think over as she walked back to the cottage. At least she knew a little more about Adam Brodie, and she felt a pang of sympathy for the bewildered child he had been, growing up in a world that, for him, had been torn apart and could not be put back together again. No wonder he was slow to trust people.

But she could not agree with James's final remark on the subject. Jessica was becoming certain that Adam's main interest in Rowan Cottage was on Ishbel's behalf, and he found Jessica a nuisance because of her stubbornness. Well, he would have to wait. She could be as difficult as he was, if she wanted to.

There was still time to go to town and start looking for a suitable dress for the dance. She changed into a sleeveless pink tunic dress patterned with white, brushed the tangles from her hair so that it hung smoothly to her shoulders and then flicked out in a curl, and went out to the car.

She had expected to spend at least two days trying to find something suitable to wear, but to her surprise she came across the perfect dress in the second shop she visited, a small boutique tucked away in a narrow street near the river.

'Lovely, isn't it?' the salesgirl asked as Jessica pirouetted before the mirror. The dress was in a soft black material that allowed the long skirt to swirl mistily about her legs as she moved. The bodice was low-cut, exposing her rounded breasts nestled into gathered cups above a long fitted waist. Narrow lacy straps fastened at the back of the neck. It was the most sophisticated dress Jessica had ever tried on, and she hesitated, dazed by the picture in the mirror before her, wanting the dress, but afraid that it was not right for her.

'You suit it,' the assistant said encouragingly, seeing the hesitation.

'Mmmm.' Jessica looked at her own slim,

smooth shoulders, at the curves of creamy breasts rising from the black lace. 'You don't think it's too——?'

'Not with your figure,' the girl said enviously, smoothing her own plump hips. 'It's perfect on you. I wish I could wear something like that.'

Jessica viewed her mirrored body with new interest. Up until then she had only been interested in making sure that clothes fitted, and that she suited the colours. But this dress—she lifted a fold of the full, flared skirt between her fingers and released it, letting it drift down like a fall of black snow—this dress was for David. And this dress showed her slender, shapely figure off to advantage. Yes, David would approve.

'It's for the dance on Friday,' she told the salesgirl, who nodded.

'I'd say that it's just right for the occasion. The annual dance is always a bit formal. We've got the dress in white, if you'd like to try it on——'

White. Party-dress white. Little-girl white. Jessica looked back at the mirror, at the elegant young woman in the black dress, and made her mind up. This dress would show Adam Brodie that she was an adult.

'I'll take it.'

Her lips were curved in a satisfied smile when she left the shop. Now she was looking forward to going to the dance with David, confident that he would not be ashamed of her. She bought shoes and a bag, made a hairdresser's appointment for Friday, then glanced at her watch and found that she still had time to go to Adam's office and have a look at the jewellery he was keeping for her. She had no jewellery of her own with her, and something among Great-aunt Kate's collection might be suitable for the dance.

She located the office after a while, and hurried up the steep stairs to the outer office. It was empty, and after waiting for a few moments, Jessica realised that the desk was neat, as though the receptionist had gone home for the day.

She hesitated, then decided that Adam must still be in his office, as the outer door was unlocked. Slowly, almost apologetically, she made her way along the short, dim corridor.

She had almost reached the door when she heard voices, and realised that Adam was not alone. Jessica turned to the outer office again, then stopped as she heard her own name spoken in a clear, musical voice that could only belong to Ishbel Stevenson.

'Well?' Ishbel prodded as Jessica stood outside. 'Have you said anything to her yet?'

Adam sounded exasperated. 'Ishbel, the girl's just arrived in Broominch! Give her time to draw breath before you start hounding her!'

'I am not hounding her—what a ridiculous way to put it! I am merely asking if you've put in my bid for Rowan Cottage.'

'I will, in due course.'

'In due course?' Ishbel laughed abruptly. 'If you don't speak to her soon, darling, then I will. I want to make it clear that I've made a definite offer. She might sell it to someone else, and I——'

'Ishbel!' his voice was hard. 'I told you that I don't want you to bother Jessica—Miss Taylor—about the cottage. You made a nuisance of yourself as far as Miss Ogilvie was concerned. Leave things to me!'

'I'm beginning to wonder if you really want me to get the place,' Ishbel said sulkily. The door was open very slightly, enough to let Jessica glimpse a section of the room, though she could not see Adam or Ishbel. She wanted to move quietly back to the outer office, to get right out on to the street again, but on the other hand she felt the need to stay where she was, a reluctant eavesdropper.

'And what does that mean?'

'It means that I'm beginning to wonder whether you're really anxious for Jessica to sell. It seems to me that you want her to stay here, in Broominch.'

'For heaven's sake! The girl's a liability as far as I'm concerned, and I'm as eager as you are to get the matter settled. Why should I want her to stay? But I'm not prepared to let any client of mine be browbeaten into doing what you want, Ishbel. And I'm not going to take my orders from you!'

'Don't talk as though it's a sudden whim,' a coquettish, coaxing note had crept into the girl's voice. She moved into Jessica's view, her back to the door. 'You know as well as I do that Rowan Cottage belongs to my family.'

A tremor ran through Jessica, and she found herself leaning towards the partly-opened door, listening intently.

'Not any more. It belonged to Kate Ogilvie legally, and you know it, Ishbel. She bought it from your grandfather, and she had the right to decide what was to become of it.'

'But that was a formality! It's on our land—it's ours!' Ishbel insisted. 'He should never have sold it—and for such a paltry amount! And your father should never have allowed him to do it!'

'That's enough, Ishbel——' But Adam's voice was drowned out in a flow of words from Ishbel.

'Just because they felt sorry for her! She should have had the decency to go back to her own people after my grandfather died. Discarded mistresses should have the sense to get out of the road when they're no longer needed.'

'Ishbel!' Adam moved into view, lunging round the end of his large desk. Papers slipped from its crowded surface as he caught the girl's shoulders and shook her. His face was dark with anger, but Ishbel, far from being intimidated, slipped her arms about his neck. Jessica, her mind reeling from the words she had just heard, watched without interest as Ishbel's fingers buried themselves in Adam's hair and she drew him down to her.

'Darling, I know you don't like me to talk about it, but if you don't want to think of the past, think about the present—the future. Our future, Adam. If I get the cottage, it means that David and Mother won't be around all the time. It can be just us—just you and me, alone. Oh, darling——'

Adam's fingers tensed on her shoulders, as though to push her away, then her arms tightened about his neck and her lips found his. After a moment his arms moved round her slim body, almost against his will.

Jessica closed her eyes, pressing the back of one hand tightly against her mouth. She was rooted to the spot, and yet she had to get away. She had heard enough—perhaps too much. She took a deep breath and opened her eyes again. Just then Adam Brodie lifted his head and looked straight at her.

Jessica ducked back, hoping that he had not seen her through the crack in the door. As quietly as she could, she inched the short distance back to the reception area, and would have gone on downstairs if she hadn't dropped her bag. She scooped it up as footsteps came along the corridor. She could not get out now without being seen. There was nothing for her to do but stay where she was, trying to look as though she had just arrived from the street outside.

CHAPTER FIVE

ISHBEL swept into the reception area and stopped short as she saw Jessica standing there. Adam, just behind her, raised one eyebrow in mild surprise.

'I—I was waiting for your secretary——' her voice trailed away under his clear gaze. He could have seen her earlier, but it was more likely that he hadn't. The door had only been opened a crack, and she had been standing in the dark hallway.

His voice was pleasant enough. 'She left early. Dentist's appointment. Can I help you?'

She took a deep breath. 'You said that you had my great-aunt's jewellery here.'

'Oh, yes. Well, I was about to close the office,' he looked down at Ishbel, then back at Jessica. 'Is it urgent?'

'No. I was in town, and I just thought I'd look in.'

'If tomorrow would do——?'

'Oh, we could spare some time just now, darling,' Ishbel chimed in, her lovely face animated as she smiled at Jessica. There was not a trace of the anger she had shown a few minutes earlier. 'We could—have a talk——'

Jessica and Adam realised at the same moment what she meant. As Jessica reached for the handle of the outer door Adam grasped Ishbel's arm. 'No, we couldn't,' he said abruptly. 'Work's over for the day. And you're the one who complained because I wasn't ready when you arrived, remember?'

'There's no hurry,' Jessica said, almost at the same time, and felt the colour rushing to her face. They went downstairs and stood in an uncomfortable group on the pavement for a few minutes as Ishbel chattered about the forthcoming dance.

'Come on, Ishbel,' Adam said firmly, at last. 'Time we were going. Can I offer you a lift, Jessica?'

'I've got my car, thanks.' She felt quite faint with relief as they walked away, Ishbel's arm through Adam's.

She had to give her full attention to the road during the drive home, still unused to its curves and corners. The enforced discipline kept her thoughts away from the discussion she had just overheard, and she was grateful for the respite. Back at the cottage she tried on her dress before the full-length mirror in the bedroom. Away from the soft lighting of the dress-shop, it still looked and felt special. Jessica grinned at her reflection.

'They'd never recognise you in the classroom!' she told herself, and her spirits rose a little. She put the dress away carefully and changed into her old jeans and a tee-shirt. There was still time to do some work in the garden, and she needed the soothing contact with earth and flowers.

As she worked outside she let her mind turn to Ishbel's words. It sounded as though Rowan Cottage had been some sort of gift to Great-aunt Kate for—well, for favours received, Jessica told herself baldly. She couldn't believe it of Great-aunt Kate! Then she remembered the inscription on the book in the cottage. After all, she only knew Kate Ogilvie as an upright, white-haired, rather stern old lady. Once, Kate had been young, vulnerable, loved and loving. Jessica wasn't shocked by what she had heard, for she believed that everyone had the right to shape their own lives. She just couldn't imagine Kate Ogilvie as anyone's mistress.

She found a watering can in the shed and made several trips to the kitchen to refill it. Watching globules of moisture sliding off leaves and nestling among petals, where they sparkled in the sun's dying rays, was a satisfying experience. When she had put the watering can back and gone indoors, Jessica could see the flowers glowing in the dusk, each plant sitting comfortably in a patch of moist dark earth. She would miss the garden when she returned to her flat.

Her muscles ached with a pleasant weariness. Jessica soaked luxuriously in a warm bath for a while before putting on a nightgown and dressing-gown. She shampooed her hair, towelled it vigorously, then tied it back loosely from her face.

Downstairs again, she put the lights on, started the fire which was ready-laid in the hearth and then, realising that she hadn't eaten for some time, opened a tin of soup and cut some sandwiches.

She had bought some paperbacks while in the town, and she settled into one of the big chairs flanking the fire and opened the first book. She became so absorbed that when she had finished her meal she carried the dishes into the kitchen and left them by the sink, returning to the sitting-room to continue her reading. With the curtains drawn and the fire crackling, the cottage was a friendly place, despite Cleo's absence. Jessica checked her watch, yawned, changed position in the comfortable chair, and decided to read one more chapter and then get to bed early. Just then, the door-knocker rattled.

Startled, she looked up from her book. It was after ten o'clock, too late for passing visitors. She half thought of staying where she was and letting the caller assume that she had gone to bed, but just then the knocker rattled again, a no-nonsense sound that threatened to continue if something wasn't done about it.

She went into the hall, remembering to switch on the porch light before answering the door.

'Adam!'

He loomed above her, unsmiling. 'I've got Cleo in the car.'

Jessica sighed. 'Adam, thanks—but no thanks. I'm all right on my own. I told your father that.'

'I know what you told my father, and I'm annoyed with him for letting you leave the dog behind when you came back here.'

'But——'

'Look what you just did,' he accused. 'You opened the door to me without stopping to ask who I was. I might have been a burglar, or a—a——'

'Oh, honestly, Adam! Do you really think that a burglar would come to the door and knock? And do you think that a burglar or a—whatever you were going to say—would tell me who they were?'

A strange expression flitted across his face. She didn't realise it, but he was trying not to laugh. The absurdity of it all had just struck him—his own pompous attitude, and Jessica's small bristling figure confronting him, barefoot and swathed in a flowered dressing-gown, her silky fair hair almost free of the ribbon tying it back. With an effort he swallowed the sudden amusement and said, 'I also brought this.'

She leaned forward to look at the box he held out. 'What is it?'

'Your aunt's jewellery. I thought you might like to have a look at it.'

'Now?'

'I had to go back to the office for something and I decided that I might as well collect the jewellery while I was there. But if it's too late——'

'No, I'd like to see it.' She stood back to let him past, then, as he ducked his head under the low door and moved into the hall, she shut the night out and led him into the warm, lamplit sitting-room.

When she came from the kitchen with coffee,

he was leafing through the book she had laid down when he arrived. 'I didn't think you'd be interested in this sort of book.'

She handed him a mug and settled herself in her armchair again. 'You thought it would be too difficult for me to understand? Even teachers can think for themselves these days.' Then she relented as colour stained his face. 'That was bitchy of me. But I do get tired of men who think that women are a brainless lot.'

He smiled, shrugging slightly. 'My fault—I don't know much about women, as you've probably realised.'

'Except Ishbel.'

He refused to be drawn. 'Ishbel isn't a reader,' he said smoothly, and changed the subject. 'There isn't much jewellery here, but what there is belongs to you. She wanted me to hand it over personally.'

Jessica slipped from the chair to the rug, and he knelt beside her, putting the box down between them before unlocking it. With gentle fingers, Jessica reached into the box and drew out a double strand of creamy pearls.

'Cultured—but quite good. Miss Ogilvie wore them a lot. There are matching ear-rings.' Adam scooped them up, delicate globes suspended from silver chains. They looked tiny in the palm of his hand. 'She rarely wore them, just the necklace. And there are some rings here.'

He passed a smaller box to Jessica, who opened it carefully. She felt as though she was prying among someone else's possessions. Adam watched her expression, sensing the thoughts that ran through her mind as she looked down at the contents of the box.

'All this jewellery meant something to her. Every piece had sentimental value. But she really wanted you to have it. She talked quite a lot about you, in the last few months.' He recalled those evenings in the cottage, the old lady talking, while he himself grew more and more intrigued with this girl she described to him. She had made him want to meet Jessica himself; perhaps, he began to realise as he watched Jessica's down-bent head, the light catching her silky hair, that was what the old lady had intended as she teased his interest in her great-niece.

Jessica lifted a heavy silver ring set with a blue stone and turned it over so that the firelight brought the jewel to life. 'I can't think why. We hardly knew each other.'

'You may be wrong. I think she sensed that you have something in common.'

'But what?' She looked up at him, pushing her hair back, and for a brief moment he recognised Kate's independence and vitality in the wide grey eyes that met his.

'Perhaps she felt that the two of you had the same outlook on life.' He picked out a broad gold band. 'I think this belonged to her mother.'

'And this?' Their heads, one fair, the other dark brown, were almost touching as they bent over the hoop of gold in Jessica's hand. The ring was broad, shaped in the pattern of twined leaves, each leaf set with three seed pearls. Adam took it from her hand and turned it over. At the back, the band was broken by three open diamond shapes revealing something that had been worked into the gold.

'Plaited hair,' he explained. 'Lovers had locks of their hair plaited, and set into friendship rings like this. It pledged their love.' He lifted the ring to the light. 'Only a hallmark—I thought there might be initials and a date.'

Before she realised what he was going to do, he had lifted her right hand and slipped the ring on to the third finger. 'It's fits!' He looked up, grinning. Now he looked relaxed and carefree, his hair slightly tousled and his eyes sparkling at her. He wore a crimson polo-necked sweater, and the colour brought out the gold glints in his hair and in his brown eyes.

Jessica looked away in confusion. 'So we do have something in common—the same hands.'

'Miss Ogilvie had beautiful hands.'

'And this was hers.' Jessica took the ring off and put it back in the box. 'It's special—not for anyone else to wear. I'll keep it, but I won't wear it.'

There were two gold chains, a sparkling jet necklace, a cameo brooch, and an old fob watch still left in the box, as well as a bracelet in a small box of its own. The bracelet was made of fine gold, beautifully engraved in a lacy pattern, with a gold safety chain to guard against loss. This time, when Adam slipped it on her wrist, Jessica did not take it off.

'It's lovely—so delicate——'

'It looks as though it had been made just for you.' He took the watch from the box. 'I don't know if this will ever go again.'

'It doesn't matter. It's lovely just as it is.' Jessica gazed at the engraved silver case, the watch face decorated in gold, pink and blue, the letters forming their own delicate pattern round the dial. 'I envy people who used to wear such beautiful things.'

'One more item.' He brought out a flat black case and handed it to her. She opened it and caught her breath. 'Oh, Adam! They're beautiful!'

The interior of the case was lined with black velvet and held a necklace, bracelet, ring and earrings in gold, set with stones that glinted deep, rich red in the light.

'What are they? Rubies?'

'No.' He took the necklace from the box and draped it over his fingers, turning his hand so that the firelight caught the stones. 'I think they're garnets. Too dark for rubies. I've never seen these before. Miss Ogilvie certainly never wore them in my presence. Here——'

She bent her head obediently, the soft hair slipping forward. She felt his fingers brush against the nape of her neck as he fastened the necklace. When she lifted her head again her eyes were bright.

'Well?'

He looked at the delicate gold lying against her creamy throat, at the dark red stones gleaming back at him. 'Lovely. Not what the average person wears with a flowered dressing-gown, of course, but nevertheless——'

She laughed, and the necklace glittered. 'Fashions have to be set by someone, haven't they? Garnets, you said?'

'Mmmm,' he said absently, frowning at the necklace. Then he snapped his fingers. 'Of course—garnets. Your great-aunt's birthday was in January, and garnets were her birthstones.'

Jessica's eyes widened. 'But my birthday's in January!'

'You see? You're finding more and more in common with her after all,' he teased. He hadn't felt so relaxed for months—not since the last time he had talked with Kate Ogilvie, he realised with a small shock. It might be the cottage itself that put him at his ease, but on the other hand, it might be the company——

Jessica, intent on trying on the bracelet, ring and ear-rings, hadn't noticed the puzzled look on his face. She put the rest of the jewellery back into its box, her mind busy with her own thoughts.

'Adam, did my great-aunt leave any papers?'

'What sort of papers? I've got the house deeds, insurance papers, will, that sort of thing.'

'Personal papers. Diaries, letters——'

There was a brief pause before he said, 'Your great-aunt knew that she was dying, Jessica. She had time to destroy anything that she wanted kept private.'

'So there was nothing? Obviously she trusted you, and I thought that perhaps she had——'

'There was a bundle of letters. She kept them with her and made me promise that they would be destroyed when—when she died.'

'And you did?' When he nodded, she went on, 'Do you know who they were from?'

'No. I took the bundle and I destroyed them at once, without looking at them. As you say, she trusted me.'

Jessica got up to move restlessly round the room. 'She was such a private person! I can't get to know her!'

'Of course you know her. She's all around you; the way she furnished this cottage, the flowers chosen for the garden, the jewellery that suits you as it suited her.'

'I wish there was something else. A letter, a diary—anything that would make her more of a person to me.'

'She believed in privacy, and that was what I liked most about her. She respected other people's right to live their own lives, and only asked that they should do the same for her.'

'I can see why you liked her. You're a very private person yourself.'

He gazed into the half-filled coffee mug on the hearth beside him, then said tersely, 'It's the only way not to get hurt.'

She smiled, moving to sit in the armchair. 'I think we've had this sort of conversation before. Adam, what do you know about Kate Ogilvie? Why was she here—in Broominch?'

This time the silence lasted for so long that she thought he was not going to answer. He finished his cooling coffee in one gulp, put the mug back on the hearth, and stared into the fire before saying, 'So you were there long enough to hear what Ishbel said this afternoon. I had wondered.'

Colour burned her face. 'I didn't think I had been seen.'

Adam rose to his feet. 'I could hardly miss seeing you, in that pink dress. But I didn't know how long you had been——'

'Spying?'

'I didn't say that. Presumably you came to the door with the intention of speaking to me. Then you heard—what did you hear, Jessica?'

'I heard Ishbel calling Kate a discarded——'

'Ishbel should think before she speaks.' He shrugged, a slight lifting of his broad shoulders. 'I suppose you won't rest now until you know the story.'

'I think I know it already. Kate Ogilvie and Ishbel's grandfather were——'

'Lovers.' Adam dropped the word lazily into the space between them. 'Lovers, Jessica. Two people genuinely in love with each other.'

'But he was already married.'

'He was divorced. Oddly enough, your great-aunt could not bring herself to marry a divorced man. It went against all that she had been taught in her youth.'

'And yet——'

Adam paused for a moment, looking her over thoughtfully. 'And yet, she cared enough to want to live here, in Rowan Cottage, so that they could see each other every day. Long before he died he sold the cottage to her for a nominal price, to make it all legal. Which was just as well, because when Ishbel grew up she wanted the place for herself.'

'Why did Kate stay on after he died?'

His voice took on an exasperated note. 'Her friends were here, as well as her memories. Just because this is a small community north of the Border, Jessica, it doesn't mean that we're a bunch of prudes. Kate was loved and respected; she got on well with everyone, including the Stevensons. Perhaps she felt that she would get more understanding from us than from her own people.' He was watching her closely. 'What do you think, Jessica?'

'So you feel as though she did the right thing?' She answered his question with one of her own.

'I know nothing about love. But I admire Kate Ogilvie for sticking to her principles—and staying on in Rowan Cottage, where she wanted to be.'

Jessica rose, turning away from his clear, steady eyes. She put a hand to her throat, and felt the hard, cold garnet necklace there. 'But Ishbel hated her! I heard her this afternoon, remember?'

He moved swiftly. Strong fingers caught at her shoulders, spun her round. His face was alive with anger, and all at once he seemed to be a stranger, dominating and yet exciting in a way that caught at her breath.

'Eavesdroppers never hear the truth! Ishbel's more of a prude than the rest of us, I'll grant you—at least, where other people are concerned. She criticises too quickly. But she got on well enough with Kate. She was resentful when she decided that she wanted Rowan Cottage and your great-aunt refused to sell it, or to undertake to leave it to Ishbel. There was no hatred, only sulkiness. Ishbel's a spoiled brat, intent on getting her own way, that's all.'

'And she wants Rowan Cottage.'

'I'm not going to start talking about that just now,' he said levelly. 'You want to take all summer to think thinks over, and you'll get it. The cottage is yours, and Ishbel can't do a thing about it.'

She looked up at him. 'What do you want me to do, Adam?'

His brows drew together. 'When you've made a decision, I'll follow whatever instructions you give me, of course.'

'I asked what you wanted me to do. Do you want me to give it to Ishbel and get out? To stop being a liability to you?'

The word hit home. A variety of expressions flitted over his face as he stared down at her. She felt a tingle run through her body as his fingers tightened on her shoulders—then he stood back, dropping his hands to his sides. 'As I said, listeners sometimes hear things that should never have been voiced,' he said coldly, formally, and picked up the coffee mugs. While he was in the kitchen Jessica put the jewellery box into the writing bureau. She slipped off the garnet bracelet, ring and ear-rings, and started to unfasten the necklace.

'About Cleo——' Adam said from the kitchen door.

'I told you, I'd rather be on my own.' Her hair twined round her fingers as she tried to unfasten the necklace. 'Could you unfasten this before you go, please?'

He lifted the soft hair aside, its fresh, clean scent filling his nostrils. As his fingers touched her neck the tremor ran through Jessica again. The catch loosened, and she caught the necklace and put it on the bureau. She began to move away from him, but he stopped her, turned her to face him, and pulled her into his arms, holding her against his hard chest as though he would never let her go again.

Then his mouth claimed hers fiercely, kindling a glow that spread slowly, deliciously through her body. They merged into each other, and his kiss had a blinding intensity that made Jessica feel that she had been born just for that moment. When he finally lifted his head from hers, he kept his arms about her, looking down at her with brown eyes that said what he could not put into words.

She answered in the only way she could, running her mouth along the strong angle of his chin, tangling her fingers in his thick soft hair until he pulled her close again, his mouth drifting over her closed eyes, her throat, then back to claim her lips in a kiss that seared fire through every part of her. She felt the strength of him as he crushed her against him, and there was sweet pain when he caught her hair in one hand and dragged her head back so that he could move his lips down the curve of her throat.

The dressing-gown was roughly pushed aside as his kisses travelled from throat to shoulder. Time and place had ceased to exist for Jessica—she wanted nothing but this moment, wanted nobody but Adam. She had never experienced such passion and longing before. Her hands moved across his broad back, aware of the warmth of his body beneath the light sweater he wore.

'Jessica,' his voice was thick with his need for her, 'I've been waiting for such a long time——'

She stopped him with her lips. Words weren't needed in this magic world that they had suddenly discovered together.

She had no idea of how long they were wrapped in each other's arms. Adam lifted her, carried her to the rug before the fire, and they sank on to its warm softness together. Jessica knew, somewhere in the mists of her mind, that this moment was a transparent bubble, and that bubbles must eventually burst. Yet she was unprepared for the moment when Adam pulled away from her, and she felt the warmth of the log fire on her bare shoulder. She reached her arms out to draw him back, but he was kneeling above her, getting to his feet, pushing tousled hair back from his face with blind gestures.

'I'm—I'm sorry—I shouldn't have——'

She got up as he made for the door. 'Adam? What is it?'

His back tensed under her fingers, then he swung round on her. The love in his eyes had been replaced by bright, hard anger. 'What is it?' He waved an arm towards the rug where they had lain in each other's arms. 'Good God, Jessica, do you need to ask? It's all wrong!'

She was suddenly aware that her dressing-gown had been pulled open, and hurriedly closed it over the low-cut nightdress. 'I don't understand! Surely you owe me an explanation?'

There was disgust now, in his look and in his voice. 'Do you really need an explanation? You know what they say—history always repeats itself! Well, not to me—I won't let it!'

Colour flamed into her face as the words hit her. Like great-aunt, like great-niece, a voice sniggered in her head. She remembered Ishbel's scornful 'discarded mistress!'

Before she could stop herself she had slapped Adam as hard as she could. He stepped back, one hand flying to his reddened cheek.

'You——!' he said between his teeth, then she cried out as he caught her by the shoulders and shook her. She was helpless in his grip, as defenceless as a kitten, and when he released her abruptly, she had to catch at the back of a chair for support.

The front door slammed, the car engine raced and then roared off into the distance, carrying Adam Brodie away from Rowan Cottage.

Jessica stared at herself in the mirror above the writing-bureau. Her mouth looked full and soft, and still throbbed from the passion of his kisses. Her treacherous body glowed from the fire his touch had lit within her. Tears rose in her eyes, sparkling on the lashes like the jewels Great-aunt Kate had left her.

Her heart contracted painfully as she remembered the disgust in Adam's eyes, the contempt in his voice. History repeating itself, he called it. Kate, loving a man who had been married to someone else, and therefore could never belong to her. And Jessica . . .

She moved slowly to the fireside chair, and sat down, staring at the glowing logs. She forced herself to conjure up pictures of Adam, laughing with Ishbel in the lounge bar at the hotel, walking with Ishbel's hand through his arm, kissing Ishbel in his office.

Jessica could admit the truth to herself, no matter how much it hurt. She loved Adam Brodie, loved him deeply, and had loved him from the first, despite—or, perhaps, because of— the stormy, passionate inner man hidden behind a cool, shuttered front.

She had been taken aback by the truth about Great-aunt Kate and Ishbel's grandfather. It hadn't fitted in with her memory of Kate Ogilvie. But now, sitting in Kate's cottage, she understood. Kate had been deeply, passionately in love, and had stayed with the man she cared for.

But Adam belonged to Ishbel. He had made it clear that he was not interested in an affair with Kate's great-niece.

Jessica realised, bleakly, that she had no choice. She had to give up Rowan Cottage, to go home, to leave Adam where he belonged.

Her love, like Kate's, was hopeless. But even
with hundreds of miles between them, even
knowing that she would never see Adam again,
Jessica sensed that she would not be able to stop
thinking of him, and wanting him.

CHAPTER SIX

JESSICA wandered barefoot round the sunny garden on the following morning as she waited for the kettle to boil.

It was a beautiful day, and the thought of leaving Rowan Cottage at once, a decision she had made before finally falling asleep the night before, dismayed her. By the time she had finished breakfast and washed the dishes she had convinced herself that she should stay in Broominch for a few weeks longer, as she had originally planned. Then Rowan Cottage would be sold—probably to Ishbel.

Jessica avoided brooding on her feelings for Adam. There was no denying that he roused her in a way nobody ever had—or ever would, if she was honest about it. But her love for him was useless—a madness that would, somehow, have to be forgotten. They would not be thrown into each other's company for much longer, she reminded herself, and tried to ignore the ache in her heart. It would be silly to run away from him. She had never run from anything before, and wasn't going to start now.

And there were other men in the world; one of them not all that far away. She had just decided to stop pining for Adam and what might have been when the door-knocker banged. She jumped, then laughed at herself. David Stevenson was on the doorstep, handsome in light slacks, a blue shirt and a blazer.

'I've been very well behaved,' he began as soon as the door opened.

'Have you?'

'Very.' He leaned against the door-frame, smiling teasingly down at her. 'I haven't come near you, or made a pest of myself, have I? Left you alone to settle in, just as you asked. And it's time for my reward. Come and have lunch with me.'

Still angry with herself for hoping that Adam was her visitor, she stared up at David. 'Oh—sorry, I was thinking about something else.'

White teeth gleamed in an amused smile. 'You really know how to make me feel wanted, Jessica! Now you owe me a date to make up for it.'

She was about to think up some excuse, but stopped. David's company was probably just what she needed to shake herself free from her turmoil over Adam. She smiled up at him. 'I'd love to have lunch with you.'

'At last! Now, there's a nice new place opened just outside the town, and I thought that afterwards I'd take you for a drive.'

He waited in the open sports car outside the gate while she hurried to get ready. His blue eyes looked her up and down when she came down the path, slim and cool in a white dress with three-quarter-length sleeves and a pattern of dark green ivy leaves forming a deep border round the flared skirt.

'You look—well, you look good enough to eat. However, I'll settle for a steak and your company.'

The restaurant he took her to was in a modernised mansion, with a view from the dining-room windows of smooth green lawns, dotted with clumps of multi-coloured azaleas. The room was half full, and held the soft hum of voices. It was just the place for a leisurely meal.

David talked during the meal about himself and his work, his family and Broominch, filling in small details about the place.

By the time the coffee had arrived, they were laughing together easily, having found a shared sense of humour. Jessica was grateful for his relaxed friendship, his willingness to accept her as she was, without the unspoken criticism she had found in Adam.

As though responding to her thought, two men rose to leave from a table at the other side of the room, in Jessica's view. One was elderly and balding; the other, who had his back to her table, was heart-wrenchingly familiar—tall, with broad shoulders and soft thick hair that was neatly brushed back.

David turned in his chair, following her gaze, as Adam swung round. Cool brown eyes swept over Jessica, Adam nodded in answer to David's wave, and then he was escorting his companion from the room without another glance.

'He might have come over to say hello,' David said casually. 'Strange type, Adam—he can be offhand when he wants to be. A business lunch, I suppose. That's why I didn't stop to talk to him when we arrived.'

'I didn't see him when we arrived,' Jessica sipped at her coffee without tasting it.

'Didn't you? You walked right past him.'

She set the cup down, and added sugar that she didn't want. Not content with throwing herself at the man the evening before, she had seemingly ignored him when she and David arrived for lunch. No wonder he had looked at her coldly!

'You look a bit flustered,' David's voice intruded. 'It isn't old Adam, is it? You haven't fallen for him?'

'Don't be silly—I hardly know him!'

'I hardly know you, but I think you're really something.' David's voice was suddenly quiet, intimate. His hand reached across the table to cover hers.

'David, I think you're the sort of man who says that to every girl you have lunch with.'

He grinned. 'Not quite. But I do appreciate a lovely woman, whereas Adam—well, I don't know what Ishbel sees in him.'

Adam's arms were about her all at once, his lips warm on her throat—Jessica forced her thoughts back to David, who was still talking and hadn't noticed anything. 'I think she's looking for a father figure. Well, let's stop wondering about them, and think about ourselves. Now I'm going to take you for a long drive, and I'm going to try to persuade you

to pitch your tent permanently in Broominch.'

'I thought you were supposed to persuade me
to go, so that your sister can buy Rowan
Cottage.'

He laughed, shrugging his shoulders. 'Aren't
you sharp! That's what she'd like me to do, but
she's on her own, now that I've met you. My
mission in life is to make sure that you stay as
near me as possible. And England's too far
away!'

They spent the afternoon exploring the rich,
rolling green countryside David knew so well and
Jessica was just beginning to appreciate. They
drove along narrow tree-lined roads, past
cottages, fields, more cottages. They walked
round a small loch that dreamed, alone, beneath
the sun. They followed the course of a broad,
lazy river that wound its way through a small
valley, and they climbed half-way up a gently-
sloping hill and sat on conveniently-placed rocks,
Jessica's hair blowing across her face. She felt
happy again, basking in the warmth of David's
admiration.

They had tea and home-made scones in a small
farmhouse tea-room at the end of the afternoon,
then drove back to Broominch.

'Come up to the house and have a drink,' he
suggested as they neared the cottage, but Jessica
shook her head.

'No thanks—I feel too untidy and windswept
to visit anyone just now.'

'I think you look marvellous, just as you are,'

he argued, but drove to the cottage without trying to persuade her.

'I had a really lovely time,' she said sincerely when he stopped the car.

'So did I. And I'm looking forward to tomorrow evening even more, now.' He reached over, touched her face with gentle fingers, then tilted her chin and kissed her lightly on the lips.

'Just practising,' he told her with a grin when they drew apart. There was a scurry and a thump outside the car, and he grimaced. 'Don't look now, love, but we're not alone.'

He got out of the car, fending off Toby's boisterous welcome and Cleo's more sedate greeting, and came round to open Jessica's door as Adam Brodie reached the car. He called the younger dog back, but David was already in control, holding Toby back so that all the dog could do to show his pleasure at seeing them was to lick every hand he could reach.

For once, Jessica welcomed the dog's attentions, glad to have an excuse not to meet Adam's clear gaze at first. He must have seen David kissing her in the car, she realised, but no doubt he had interpreted it as Jessica kissing David!

'Sorry we didn't get a chance to talk during lunch.' David leaned against the car. 'We decided not to intrude, as it seemed to be a business lunch.'

'Yes, it was. And you two seemed to be intent on each other—so I didn't interrupt.' Adam's voice was quiet and even, but Jessica was acutely aware, when she finally looked up, that his eyes were hard as they travelled over David, and then over her own face.

'We were,' David agreed cheerfully, catching Jessica's hand in his own. 'We had a terrific day, didn't we?'

She let her fingers stay in his. 'Wonderful,' she agreed lightly, her gaze on Adam's face. He met the challenging look and held it. Finally, she had to look away.

'I thought I'd walk the dogs in this direction, just in case there was anything you needed,' he said smoothly. 'But obviously you're managing— very well.'

If there was an underlying note of sarcasm in his voice, David didn't notice it. 'She's managing very well,' he confirmed breezily. 'As a matter of fact, I'm trying to coax her to stay in the village. We need someone like Jessica to brighten the place up. Don't you think so, Adam?'

There was a brief pause, then, 'I think it's up to Jessica to decide what she wants to do,' Adam said carefully.

'So you don't care either way?'

Adam called sharply to Toby, who was sniffing contentedly through the grass verge, and the dog went to him at once, his tail between his legs. 'I'm Jessica's lawyer, David—that's all. Caring doesn't come into it.' His fingers kneaded the young dog's neck, as though apologising for the spurt of anger which had, unfairly, been unleashed on Toby. 'Well, I'd better move on, the dogs are getting bored.'

'I'll have to go, too. I'll pick you up tomorrow evening, Jessica, and we'll all meet in the bar for a drink before going into the dance, okay?'

David released Jessica's hand, but stayed where he was as though hoping that Adam would move away and leave them alone. But Adam lingered, and it was Jessica who turned to the gate and left them to go their separate ways.

As she closed the door she remembered Adam's words to Ishbel, 'The girl's a liability as far as I'm concerned.' Her lips tightened. Let him think that she was an empty-headed flirt—let him disapprove of her friendship with David. Adam's opinion no longer mattered. Ishbel was welcome to him.

But somehow, it was hard to believe her own thoughts.

She spent most of Friday preparing for the dance. On a sudden impulse, she decided to have her hair styled at the same time as having it cut, and was pleased with the result—a soft, shining cap fringed across her forehead and gently curling round her face, emphasising her neat features and wide eyes.

Later, she spent more time than usual at the dressing-table mirror, using blue eye-shadow and liner to give added depths and lustre to her eyes, applying a light touch of blusher along her high cheekbones, carefully outlining her lips with a new red lipstick, a change from her usual pale pink. Then, at last, she slipped on the black dress and stood before the long mirror.

She hardly recognised herself. Her face, framed by fair curls, was animated. The dress and hair-style showed off her long, slender neck to advantage, and gave added grace to her smooth shoulders and arms. Her breasts peeped from the soft material, and the dress hugged her slim waist and rounded hips before cascading to the floor like a black waterfall.

There was only one thing missing. She went downstairs to collect Great-aunt Kate's jewel-case. The pearls looked good against the black dress, but didn't, Jessica felt, suit her skin-tones. She opened the flat black box and drew out the garnets. When the ring, bracelet, necklace and ear-rings were on, she stood back and surveyed her reflection thoughtfully.

The garnets were perfect. The gold gleamed richly against the colour of her gown, and the stones themselves seemed to bring out an answering glow from her skin. She moved her head languidly, so that the studs in her ears caught the light. She looked more mature than usual; poised, self-assured, sophisticated. At last, she looked like the sort of person who could own Rowan Cottage.

David stood in the middle of the small sitting-room, darkly handsome in a deep blue suit with a white polo-necked evening sweater, and looked her over with undisguised admiration.

'Turn around,' he commanded. When she had done so, in a soft black swirl, he grinned. 'You look—well, I'm glad you're mine, and nobody else's!'

He picked up the white shawl she had decided on as a wrap, and put it about her shoulders, letting his lips brush the nape of her neck as he wrapped the lacy shawl about her. A thrill of excitement ran through her at the touch.

Adam and Ishbel were sitting at a corner table in the bar when Jessica walked in, with David behind her. Ishbel was talking and Adam, who looked superb in a black evening suit with bow tie and white ruffled shirt, listened to her, staring down at the glass he twisted ceaselessly between his fingers.

He looked up as Jessica entered, glanced at her without recognition, then blinked, rising to his feet. By the time she reached the table, his expression was politely blank, but that first admiring glance was burned into her memory.

Ishbel, like a flame in an orange dress, dominated the group and glossed over Adam's silence without seeming to notice it. With the air of someone who is used to getting good service, she beckoned a waiter, and David ordered drinks for himself and Jessica. Jessica began to get over her nervousness. She knew that she looked good, she had a very handsome and attentive escort, and it was going to be a wonderful evening. She smiled into David's blue eyes.

The dance was in progress when they arrived, and David swept Jessica into his arms and moved on to the dance floor with her as soon as they claimed a table.

'Now, this is my idea of a pleasant evening,' he told her. He was an excellent dancer, and they stayed where they were, only returning to the table when the music changed to an old-fashioned waltz.

'That's the worst of these local hops,' David grimaced. 'Every age-group, so they have to cater for all tastes. Some of those young farmers are getting a bit long in the tooth, if you ask me.'

'Perhaps you'd better let the older generation take over, then?' Adam suggested. 'Would you care to dance, Jessica?'

She wanted to refuse, but he was already on his feet, waiting for her.

'Go ahead,' Ishbel said sweetly. 'Like David, I find this dance dull.'

To Jessica's surprise, she enjoyed dancing with Adam. He held her firmly, guided her expertly around the floor, and danced very well. As they swooped past the Stevensons, Jessica saw that Ishbel was watching them closely, while David was talking to a waiter.

'You're a good dancer,' Adam murmured into her hair.

'So are you.'

'I enjoy dancing. Having a good time?'

'Mmm. David is a very entertaining escort.'

Adam's fingers tightened momentarily on hers. 'As long as you don't take him too seriously.'

She looked up, met his eyes only inches from

hers, and looked away again. 'I have no intention of taking him seriously.'

'Good.'

'Although I don't know why you felt that you had to warn me. I think he's charming.'

'Oh, he is. And you look very beautiful.'

She realised that she was blushing like a schoolgirl. 'So does Ishbel.'

'She likes to be noticed,' said Adam enigmatically, and his arm tightened about her as he swung her into a turn. Finally the music ended, and he released her and escorted her back to the table, where he immediately claimed Ishbel. She moved into his arms as though she belonged there. Jessica watched the two of them on the dance floor, Ishbel's lovely face upturned to Adam, his head bent over her, his mouth shaping itself into that amazingly warm smile he had. Jessica's throat tightened and she turned to talk to David.

A light supper was served half-way through the evening, then the older dancers began to drift away, the lights were lowered, and a casual party mood came over those who were left. The musicians swept into pop music, and the floor was crowded.

'He's still quite a dancer, is old Adam,' David said admiringly when the four of them met again at their table. Adam grinned and pushed back the lock of hair which had managed to flop over his forehead. 'It's nothing—I just like to keep up with the youth of today.'

'You wouldn't think it of him, Jessica, but he

can be the life and soul of the party when he wants to be. Even does the Cha—Charleston.' David's tongue tripped slightly over the word. 'Come on, Adam, let's see the Charleston. I'll tell them to play something suitable.' He started to get up, but Adam shook his head.

'I only dance that when I've had a lot to drink.'

'That,' said David cheerfully, 'is no problem at all. Waiter——'

'Not for me. I think you're drinking enough for both of us,' Adam said calmly, but his eyes were watchful as they surveyed the younger man. The waiter arrived, and while David and Adam argued over the order Ishbel shrugged and smiled at Jessica.

'Enjoying yourself?'

'More than I thought I would,' she admitted.

'We haven't seen you as often as I'd hoped. Do you ride, Jessica?'

'I used to, a bit. But I haven't ridden for years now.'

Interest flared into Ishbel's eyes. 'Come riding with me one day. Let's say—Sunday? The stables are shut then, but the horses still have to be exercised, and on Sunday I go where I want, instead of taking the usual trails with the learners.'

'I'd like that. But I warn you, I'm not very good.'

'If you ride as well as you dance, you'll be terrific,' David put in. 'What about you, Adam—hasn't Ishbel persuaded you to take up the sport yet?'

Adam's dark head was shaken emphatically. 'No, thank you!'

'He's a coward,' David confided in a loud stage-whisper to Jessica. It seemed to her that there was more than a touch of malice in his teasing now, but Adam didn't seem to be troubled by it.

'Perhaps,' he agreed easily. 'I like to think that I just prefer the comfort and safety of my own two feet.'

'Nonsense!' Ishbel ran one finger down the line of his jaw. 'It's perfectly safe—I haven't lost a client yet.'

He removed her hand from his face, but kept it imprisoned in his own. 'Nevertheless, just make sure that Jessica gets a nice quiet horse. She isn't used to riding, remember.'

She made a face at him then stood up, pulling him to his feet with her. 'Come and dance!'

The ear-rings began to pinch the lobes of Jessica's ears as the dance was drawing to its close. She took them off and put them on the table, where they threw ruby highlights at the glittering ball suspended over the dance floor. Ishbel's small brown hand reached out and picked one of the ear-rings up.

'Pretty. You've got a complete set, too. They look quite old.'

'They are. They were among some pieces of jewellery Great-aunt Kate left me.'

Ishbel held the ear-ring up to the light. 'What sort of stone is that?'

'Garnets, according to Adam. Her birthstone, and mine too, as it happens, so I thought——' Jessica had been looking at the dancers. When she turned back to Ishbel, she saw that the other girl's eyes were large with astonishment, realisation, and finally anger.

'Garnets? And they belonged to . . . you got them from Miss Ogilvie?' She looked quickly at David, then back at Jessica. Her eyes were bright, her face flushed. 'How could you? How could you flaunt them here, when you knew we were going to be with you? How could you?'

'But——'

David leaned forward and put one hand over his sister's hand, which had clenched itself into a fist on the table. 'Watch it, Ishbel, that's no way to speak to Jessica! What's got into you?'

Ishbel pulled her hand free, picked up the ear-ring, and held it before his eyes. 'This!' she hissed, tears brimming her dark lashes. 'The garnet set, David! Our grandmother's garnets!'

It seemed to Jessica that the music and the light ripple of voices had stopped. She half turned in her chair, seeking help from some-where—anywhere—and found it in Adam, who was standing some distance away talking to a group of people.

He happened to glance in her direction as she turned, and their eyes met. The smile left his face, and he said something to the people he was with and came back to the table in time to hear Ishbel say again:

'How could you do this to me?'

'But I don't——'

Adam's hand dropped lightly on Ishbel's shoulder, and stayed there as he moved to sit by her side. 'Ishbel, what's going on?' He kept his voice low, aware of the people nearby. When she turned to him, the tears were beginning to spill from her blue eyes.

'The garnets. She's wearing the garnets that belonged to my grandmother—flaunting them in front of me——' her voice broke and she made to get up from the table. Only Adam's grip kept her where she was. He looked from one face to the other, bewildered. Ishbel was flushed with fury, while Jessica was chalk white, her grey eyes blank with shock.

'What on earth are you talking about?' There was a hint of anger now in Adam's voice. 'For heaven's sake, will someone explain it to me?'

Both David and Ishbel started to speak, but Jessica got to her feet, gathering the ear-rings from the table. 'I think I'd rather just go home,' she said through stiff lips. David jumped up to stand beside her.

'I'll take you, love.'

'I'll take her home,' Adam put in swiftly. He, too, rose to his feet, and the two men glared at each other.

'Adam, you—you can't!' Ishbel forgot her distress for a moment, clutching at Adam's sleeve. Jessica felt her head swimming, and knew that if she didn't get away from the noisy, thronged room soon she would dissolve into tears, or take the easy way out, and faint.

'You've been drinking all evening—you're not fit to drive!' Adam's voice was tight with suppressed anger.

'You don't think I'd be stupid enough to bring my car to this sort of do, surely?' David sneered. 'We came by taxi, and I'm going to phone for one now. Get your wrap, darling, I'll meet you in the foyer.' And so saying he disappeared into the crowd of dancers. Without looking at the other two, Jessica made her own way to the cloakroom, retrieved her shawl, and walked, in a trance, to the foyer. Adam was waiting for her.

'Jessica, if you'll sit down for five minutes, I'll take you home.'

'What about Ishbel?'

'I meant that I would drive you both home. David's had a fair amount to drink, and I don't think——' he began, but she cut through the words, ignoring them.

'Why didn't you tell me?'

'Tell you what?'

She felt tears crowding at the back of her eyes, and forced them away. 'Tell me about the garnets—that they belonged to Ishbel's family! Did it give you a lot of satisfaction to see me wearing them in front of her? Did it, Adam?'

He stared down at her, confused; then anger blazed across his face, drawing his dark brows together over stormy eyes. 'You don't mean to say that you thought I knew about the jewellery?'

'Of course you did—you must have done!'

He took a step towards her and she flinched back from the fury in his eyes. 'Look here, Jessica——'

A hand touched her shoulder, drew her into the circle of David's arm. 'The taxi's here,' he said. 'Come on, love, let's go.'

Adam looked from Jessica to David, opened his mouth to say something, then shrugged and turned back to the dance hall.

'Sometimes,' said David thoughtfully, 'I don't know what to make of that guy.'

Jessica rested her head briefly on his shoulder. She was too upset to care any more about Adam, or Ishbel, or the garnets. 'David, take me home—please!'

'Okay, my love. Let's go,' he said comfortingly, and led her across the foyer and out into the night, to where the taxi waited.

CHAPTER SEVEN

DAVID'S shoulder was comfortable, his silence soothing, and as Jessica got out of the taxi and looked at Rowan Cottage's familiar bulk in the night she began to recover from the first feeling of shock caused by Ishbel's outburst.

'But I still don't understand what it was all about!' she protested when they were inside the cottage and David was poking the banked-up fire into a cheerful blaze. He dropped the poker, fumbled in the hearth, and finally retrieved it.

'Hmm? Oh—the garnets. Well, they used to belong to our grandmother, as you probably gathered. You see, your great-aunt came to Broominch after my grandparents divorced, and she and the old man—well——'

'I know about them.'

'That makes it easier for me to explain,' he said with obvious relief. He got up from the hearth-rug and had to catch hold of the mantelpiece for a second to regain his balance. He had the slightly unsteady look of someone who had had too much to drink, Jessica noticed for the first time. 'She— my grandmother, that is—must have thrown the garnets in the old boy's face when she walked out, and he passed them on to Miss Ogilvie. They've been in the family for a couple of generations, which is why we'd heard of them. We thought our grandmother had taken them with her.'

Jessica shivered, moved closer to the fire. 'If I had only known—I'd never have worn them!'

'How could you know?' he asked reasonably. 'You're a stranger here.'

'But Adam could have told me. Surely he knew about them?'

David took the shawl from about her shoulders and tossed it on to a chair. 'I don't know. Perhaps he did. I must say, Jessica, they look marvellous on you.' His blue eyes seemed to glow as they travelled over her face, her throat, the glittering necklace, her shoulders, the full curve of her breasts——

'I'll make some tea,' she began, but he caught her hand as she moved towards the kitchen. 'A drink would be more acceptable.'

'I've only got sherry.'

David made a face, then grinned. 'So we can forget about the refreshments. Come and talk to me instead.'

She tried to turn towards the kitchen again, but his grip on her hand was tighter than she had realised. She felt herself being drawn closer, until she was caught within the circle of his arms.

'David——'

'Hush!' he ordered gently, and kissed her. At first she responded, then as the kiss became too intense she tried to draw back. His arms tightened about her, his lips fastened on hers with a determination that sent a flutter of alarm through Jessica. She struggled, but he paid no attention. When he finally lifted his head, her lips felt as though they had been crushed.

'I've been waiting for this moment since I first saw you,' David said huskily, and she could feel his body trembling against hers. She laughed shakily.

'David, I think it's time you went home.'

He shook his head, smiling lazily down at her. His eyes were half-closed. 'Home? My darling, we've got the rest of the night before us. I'm not going home for a long time yet,' he said, and kissed her again, a deep, long kiss.

All at once Jessica realised that Rowan Cottage was quite isolated, and that she was not nearly as strong as David, and could hardly throw him out if he didn't want to leave. She fought down a brief moment of panic and managed to pull away from him, smoothing her tousled hair.

'David, go home—please!'

He raised an eyebrow at her, mockingly. 'Come on, darling, we both know that you don't mean that.'

'I do.' Jessica tried to gather her wits together, resorting to her schoolteacher voice as she moved towards the hall door. 'I'm not in the mood to play games. I just want you to go home!'

He was at the door before her, smiling down at her with bright eyes. He looked very handsome, but she now knew that he was probably too drunk to think clearly.

'Not in the mood to play games?' he mimicked her. 'Jess, darling, that's what you've been doing since we met. Teasing me, coming out for the afternoon, looking beautiful for the dance—we're both adults, my sweet. No need to pretend. You wouldn't have worn a dress like that if you hadn't wanted to tell me something.'

His fingers caressed her shoulder, moved down to the gathered material at the top of the dress. When she slapped him the smile stayed on his face. 'You see?' David said softly, and pulled her into his arms.

His mouth bruised hers, moved to her throat, and down to the hollow between her breasts. His fingers bit painfully into her shoulders. She tried to relax, to submit to his kisses, telling herself that he would come to his senses if she stopped fighting him. But when his fingers reached behind her neck to fumble with the fastening of her dress she pushed him away with as much strength as she could find. He staggered back, caught off balance, and almost fell over a small table. A bowl of flowers was knocked over, water pooling on the table and dripping to the carpet.

'You really are playing the little innocent, aren't you?' he slurred over the words. 'Come off it, Jess. Your great-aunt was a bit of a girl herself—what makes you think you're different?'

'How dare you!' She wasn't sure whether she was shaking with fear, or anger.

David shrugged. 'Darling, you know as well

as I do why she left the place to you. A chip
off the old block. And what's wrong with that?
What's the outraged innocence all about? Think
I'm not good enough for you? Oh, darling, I
could be very good for you if you'd just——'

He moved towards her again, and Jessica
backed away. No point in screaming for help,
for there was nobody around to hear her. And
even faced with a drunk and very determined
young man she couldn't bring herself to be
melodramatic enough to scream, she knew well
enough. She had time to wonder, as he reached
for her and she managed to step out of reach, if
she had the nerve to pick up an ornament and
hit him with it. The thoughts flashed through
her head, together with mounting anger at
herself for not realising in time what sort of
situation she was walking into.

'Come on, Jess,' he coaxed, then as she half
turned in an attempt to find something she could
at least threaten him with, his hands were on her
shoulders, pulling her towards him, gathering her
triumphantly into his embrace. His lips sought
hers as she tried to turn her head away. His hands
moved over her body, while hers beat ineffectually
against his back.

Then David swung away from her so abruptly
that she almost fell against the wall, and Adam
Brodie was saying quietly, politely, 'I don't think
Jessica's very impressed, David.'

The younger man pulled free of Adam's grip,
and smoothed down his jacket. 'What the blazes
do you think you're doing in here?'

'One of you forgot to shut the front door properly. Very careless.' Adam turned to Jessica, his eyes surveying her with that shuttered, expressionless look he had. 'Are you all right?'

'Of course she's all right! Who asked you to push your way in here?' David demanded truculently. He swayed, and caught at the back of a chair.

'I just dropped in to see how things were with Jessica.'

'Things are all right!'

'I don't think she'd agree with you, David. You've had too much to drink. Why don't you go home?'

'Where's Ishbel?'

'At the farm.'

David Stevenson threw back his head and laughed. 'At home? Oh, Adam, didn't you even stop to give her a goodnight kiss? In too much of a hurry to rush down here and visit Jessica, were you?'

Adam looked him up and down, and the laughter caught in David's throat. 'David,' Adam's voice was quiet, but there was cold, biting steel in its tones, 'for the past five hours I've wanted to knock your teeth down your throat. Perhaps it would do you a lot of good. But I think Jessica's had a difficult enough time already with the Stevensons, so I'd just as soon not spread you all over her carpet. However, if you insist——'

David held out a hand hurriedly, backing

away. 'Okay—okay, no need to get stroppy about it. Jess——'

'Goodnight, David,' Adam said grimly.

'I only want to apologise!'

'Get out!' Adam opened the hall door. David smoothed his hair back, glanced from Jessica to Adam, shrugged, and walked out. Adam followed him into the hall as Jessica sank down on to a chair. She thought—she hoped—that they had both left, and looked up with a start as Adam came back into the room. He closed the door, leaned back against it, and surveyed her. Colour surged into her face beneath his expressionless gaze. She knew that her hair was a mess, and that her face must be smeared with lipstick. She put a hand to her throat, and felt the garnet necklace beneath her fingers.

'I told you that you should have kept Cleo,' he said quietly, at last. He went to the cupboard where the sherry was kept, and came to her side a few moments later, pushing a glass into her hand.

'Drink it.'

She drank obediently, and choked as the liquid burned her throat. 'That's not sherry!'

'Drink it all,' was the stern reply.

'Don't bully, me, Adam. I've had enough!' Even to her own ears her voice sounded sharp, nearing hysteria. 'You said it yourself, the other night.'

'I did what?'

'After we—after you'd kissed me! History repeating itself, you said! Kate Ogilvie, and now me——' She stopped. The flowers she had just lifted from the floor dropped from her fingers.

'Jessica, I——' He touched her fingers, his own hand warm and strong, then tipped her chin up so that he could see her face. 'Your hand's as cold as ice. And you're looking a bit green——'

'I don—don't—don't feel very——' she clapped a hand to her mouth, then scrambled to her feet and fled upstairs.

As she went, she heard Adam saying thoughtfully from the bottom of the stairs, 'I don't think the brandy was a very good idea after all.'

Fifteen minutes later, feeling more like herself, she came out of the bathroom to find that he had hung her dressing-gown on the door-handle.

Shakily, she took off the lovely black dress, brushed her hair, and wrapped herself in the dressing-gown. Her face, scrubbed clean of smeared make-up, was pale, and her eyes looked enormous. She thought briefly of putting on some fresh make-up, then dimissed the idea. She really didn't care what sort of picture she presented to Adam Brodie. His opinion of her couldn't sink any lower.

He was sitting in one of the big armchairs, drinking his tea, when she went downstairs. He had added logs to the fire, and it blazed cheerfully.

'All right now?'

She nodded, went to the bureau, and took out the black case. She placed the garnets in it, and handed it to Adam before sitting down and accepting the mug of tea he offered her.

'I want you to give these back to Ishbel's mother. They're hers.'

'Actually, they're yours, in the legal sense.'

'There's more to life than the legal side, Adam. You wouldn't know anything about that, but I do. Morally, they're not mine. Besides, I don't even want to see them again.'

He looked down at the case, turning it over between his large, capable hands, then slipped it into an inside pocket. 'I'd just like you to know that I knew nothing about them.'

'Honestly?'

He looked up, his eyes holding hers in a level gaze. 'Do you really think I'd have let you wear them if I'd known? You may not think much of me, but I would hardly do a thing like that to you—or to Ishbel.'

It was true. He would never have let her hurt Ishbel in public. She nodded.

'Of course you wouldn't. I'm sorry I even thought it.'

She sipped at the tea. It was hot and sweet, just what she needed. The fire's warmth felt good on her bare feet. The room had regained its usual cosy, safe appearance, and Adam seemed a part of it, relaxed in the chair across the hearth from hers, still immaculate in his dinner suit and crisp shirt.

'I was so taken aback by what happened at the dance that I didn't stop to think,' she continued.

'Ishbel was wrong to cause a scene without giving you a chance to explain things. But then,

Ishbel's—well, she's used to getting everything she wants.'

'Like Rowan Cottage, and——' Jessica bit her lip, then went on. 'You warned me about David. And I wouldn't listen.'

He moved restlessly. 'Jessica, David's not as bad as he seemed tonight. He'll feel terrible in the morning, and I don't want you to think he's anything but a young man who had too much to drink and got carried away. He enjoys being a bit of a Casanova, that's all.'

'Adam, why did you come here tonight?' She tried to catch some reaction, but his face was impassive.

'Because I knew he'd had more to drink than he could handle. I had a feeling that you two had—misunderstood each other.'

All at once she was seized with a wave of longing for him. She wanted to move across the hearth, to go into his arms and be held there, safe and warm. The feeling was so strong that she put the mug of tea down, almost dropping it, and got to her feet. Adam rose with her, his hand on her arm. 'Is anything wrong?'

'No——'She pulled her arm away. She had to get away from him, because she couldn't bear to be so near him, yet unable to touch him. 'I—I'm tired. I'd like to go to my room.'

'You could do with some sleep,' his voice was brisk, matter-of-fact. 'I'll damp the fire down and wash these for you.' He picked up both mugs and went to the kitchen door, then looked back at her. 'On you go. I'll see to things down here.'

'I'll see you out first.' Her head felt muzzy
with exhaustion and misery. Adam disappeared
into the kitchen, and she heard the faint click of
the mugs being put on the draining board. Then
he came back into the room, put his hands on her
shoulders, and in an unexpected gesture bent his
dark head and kissed her very gently on the
forehead.

'Go to bed, Jessica.' He removed his hands,
stepped back, his voice suddenly formal. 'You're
perfectly safe as far as I'm concerned.'

She knew that. And she knew that if she
tried to argue with him, she would be overtaken
by the tears that threatened to fill her eyes.
Like a child, she obediently turned and went
out of the room and carried on upstairs to bed.
Lying in the dark, she heard him moving about
downstairs.

She tossed the patchwork quilt over a chair
and lay down, covered only by a thin sheet.
The night seemed oppressive. Exhaustion swept
in on her, but she forced herself to stay awake.
Once she knew that Adam had gone, she would
sleep.

But her eyes closed of their own accord, and
she was fast asleep in a matter of minutes.

The room was filled with a dull grey light when
she woke next morning. From where she lay she
could see the sky through the windows. It looked
heavy and overcast.

She stretched, turned over, and saw the black
evening dress neatly laid over a chair. Memory

returned, and she sat up and reached for her watch. The hands showed that it was seven-thirty.

Downstairs a door opened, then closed. The latch on the garden gate clicked. She scrambled out of bed and ran to the window in time to see Adam Brodie, still wearing his dinner suit, get into the car parked by the fence. He didn't look back at the cottage.

The engine coughed, turned over, and the car eased out on to the road and went off in the direction of the village. As the engine faded, another sound was carried to Jessica on the still air—the crisp tap of hooves on tarmacadam. The animal came into sight, and Jessica recognised it as the big horse Ishbel had been putting over the jumps in the meadow. Ishbel herself, in a dark anorak and jodhpurs, her black hair beneath a riding hat, was in the saddle. She was watching the disappearing car, and then she turned, her eyes raking the cottage.

Jessica jumped back guiltily and stayed where she was until she heard the hoof-beats quicken into a trot, then a canter, finally fading into the distance, taking the route the car had followed.

Colour swept into Jessica's face as she realised what it must have looked like to the other girl. She had certainly seen and recognised Adam's car. She had possibly seen Adam himself, still in the clothes he had worn the previous evening. Obviously, she would jump to the conclusion that they had spent the night together. Then the flush ebbed from Jessica's cheeks as she turned back into the room and saw that she had been warmly covered by Great-aunt Kate's patchwork quilt. But surely— she frowned, standing at the foot of the bed. She distinctly remembered throwing the quilt over the chair before going to sleep. Now the only item on the chair was the black dress— and she remembered letting it drop to the floor when she took it off and put on the dressing-gown Adam had left on the door-handle for her.

Adam! He had stayed in the house all night, probably with some vague idea of being on hand if anything happened, had come into the room while she was asleep, had covered her warmly, and had picked the dress off the floor. She shook her head in bewilderment. And now, Ishbel thought that he had stayed with her; not as a guardian, but as a lover.

Jessica ran her fingers through her hair and sighed. Just when things couldn't get worse— they did!

The kitchen and sitting-room were immaculate. A tapestry footstool on the hearth-rug between the two armchairs indicated that Adam had dozed there during the night. There was nothing else to show that he had been there.

James Brodie arrived in the middle of the morning, Cleo by his side. The sky was still heavy, and Jessica was busy with housework. She had just finished polishing the furniture when James arrived. His smiling, kindly face brightened the dull morning for her.

He sniffed appreciatively as he sat down in the sitting-room. 'The smell of polish seems to fit into a cottage better than any other sort of house.'

She ran a hand lovingly over the large table, which reflected the room back at her. 'It's like playing with a life-sized doll's house,' she confessed, laughing. 'I don't normally enjoy housework, but here, at Rowan Cottage, it's a pleasure. I'll be sorry when I have to let the place go.'

'So you're going to sell?' James picked up her remark when she came back with a tray of coffee and biscuits. Cleo nosed around the room then settled on the rug, contentedly.

'My work is in England, my home is in England.'

'What about that idea you had of finding work here?'

'A lovely dream, that's all.'

James's level gaze was so like his son's that she had to look away, bending to make a fuss of the dog. 'You like this place, don't you?'

'I love it. I just seem to be an upsetting influence, though. The sooner I'm away from Broominch, the better for everyone here.'

'A pretty face like yours couldn't upset anyone. I've been instructed, by the way, to bring Cleo back and leave her with you, no matter what you say.' He looked thoughtfully at her. 'I got the impression that Adam didn't want to bring her back himself. He looked very tired and very grim when he left for the office this morning. I take it that the dance was not a success?'

The story poured out. It seemed to Jessica that having talked about the garnets and Ishbel's reaction, she had to go on and tell him about the scene with David. She didn't tell Adam's father that his son had spent the night in the cottage, or that Ishbel had seen him leaving, but she had an idea that James Brodie was shrewd and observant enough to know when his son had returned home.

'Come and have some lunch with me. I know of a nice wee restaurant near Broominch, and I'm always glad of an excuse to go there,' he said abruptly when she had finished her story. 'I think you need to be dined in style.'

They went in Jessica's car, because James had walked from his house with the dog. She wore the burgundy-coloured suit with a high-necked black sweater beneath it, and James looked across the table at her with satisfaction when they had ordered their meal.

'I enjoy eating when I've got an attractive companion,' his eyes twinkled at her. 'Nowadays, that seldom happens. Kate and I dined out occasionally, dressed in all our finery. A very attractive woman, was Kate. You remind me of her.'

'A chip off the old block?' Jessica suggested, an edge in her voice as she thought of David's words the evening before. But James didn't seem to notice.

'In a way. Kate was independent, and practical. I think she made a good choice when she left the cottage to you. She loved the place and she wanted it to go to someone who would appreciate it.' He paused while the waitress put plates before them, then said slowly and deliberately when the girl had left them, 'That's why she wouldn't agree to sell to Ishbel.'

'I don't see why she objected. After all, it will almost certainly go to Ishbel now.'

'Not until and unless you say so. And that's why I'm going to ask you to hang on to it.'

She stared at him, taken aback. 'But why should you ask me that?'

'You like the cottage, don't you? You like Broominch, don't you? And yet you're letting yourself be driven away because of a spoiled lassie and a handful of jewels. I thought Kate's great-niece would have more go in her than that!'

'But—just because she didn't want Ishbel to get the place, it doesn't mean that I have to keep it,' Jessica protested.

'You owe it to her, girl,' the old man admonished her. 'Do you think she'd have left the place to you if she didn't think you'd care about it? Mebbe you didn't see much of each other, but Kate thought highly of you. You were the only one she'd trust with Rowan Cottage. It's your heritage, and if you've not got the determination to hold on to it until you're good and ready to sell then you're no relation to Kate Ogilvie!'

He pushed his plate back and stared challengingly at her. Again, she was sharply reminded of Adam's straightforward look.

'It's not just Ishbel. It's—well, I feel that I'm just getting in the way here. I'd rather go back to England.'

'Is it Adam's moods that bother you? Lassie, don't let him force you away either,' James dismissed his son with a wave of the hand. 'There's no knowing half the time what's in that head of his. And he likes you well enough, though you might not think it. He's daft about his dogs, and he'd not let Cleo stay with anyone he couldn't trust.'

While Jessica was still trying to decide whether that was a compliment or not, James's hand reached across the table to cover hers briefly. 'And mebbe I should ask you to stay on in Broominch for a wee while longer for Adam's sake as well. Rowan Cottage was a refuge for him at times, when he didn't want to be under the same roof as me, and Ishbel was pestering him. Kate knew how to deal with Adam. And you're like her, as I said.'

Jessica forced a smile, blinking tears away. 'If you're matchmaking, I'd better warn you that Adam isn't interested in me. He's going to marry Ishbel—and I don't need to be a fortune-teller to know that!'

He laughed. 'Mebbe so, mebbe so. We'll wait and see if you're right. Adam'll do what's best for himself when the time comes, I've no doubt of that. But Kate and I always knew that Ishbel wasn't the right one for him. A child, with a schoolgirl crush on him. She's got some growing up to do before she's ready to marry any man. I hope he finds that out for himself, if he hasn't realised it already. Look at it this way, Jessica.' The mischief was back in his smile, taking years off his age. 'If Ishbel Stevenson's fretting about getting her hands on Rowan Cottage, she'll mebbe stop fretting about getting her hands on Adam—so you'll do me and Kate both a kindness if you'll stay here for a few weeks more, as you planned!'

CHAPTER EIGHT

SHE should have argued, should have resented James's calm assumption that she would see things his way, but there was a charm about James Brodie that Jessica could not resist. She found herself agreeing with him, promising that she wouldn't let anyone force her into making sudden decisions about the cottage.

A huge bunch of flowers was lying on the doorstep when she got back to the cottage. A note with them read 'Called to grovel about last night, but either you aren't in, or you aren't speaking. I feel like a heel. Ishbel isn't speaking to me either. Sorry, sorry, sorry—David. P.S. Ishbel has just spoken to me. She says I have to remind you that you are going riding tomorrow 2 p.m. Sorry again—honest! David.'

Jessica laughed and shook her head as she read it. Adam was right—David was more of an idiot than a cold-blooded seducer. Then she wrinkled her brow thoughtfully over the P.S. Obviously, Ishbel intended to follow up her offer of a riding date. Was it an olive branch now that the garnets were returned? Or did she want to get an opportunity to talk about the cottage? Jessica was uncomfortably aware that Ishbel had seen Adam leaving the cottage early in the morning, and looked on that as another reason why Ishbel would dislike her, rather than offer friendship.

She inhaled the scent from the flowers, decided that she was being unnecessarily suspicious, and opened the door to a rapturous welcome from Cleo. By the time she had arranged the flowers in two vases, one for the sitting-room and one for the small hall, it had begun to rain. A soft drizzle covered the countryside in a grey veil. Jessica changed into sturdy jeans and boots, put on her anorak, and took Cleo for a long walk.

They climbed the hill behind the cottage, passing through the meadow where Ishbel's jumps gleamed in the rain, the only colourful objects in the muted green of the wet field. They went on through the belt of trees until they reached the top of the hill, where Jessica sat on a rock to catch her breath. Far below she could see the clump of trees that sheltered the cottage. To the left she could see the roofs of the Stevenson house and stables. A toy car was parked in the courtyard before the house, and she wondered if it was Adam's. He probably spent most of his spare time there, she thought bleakly, and tried to forget about him. But no man had ever stayed in her mind so persistently, and no man had ever caused that tingle that crept over her when she remembered his touch.

'There are always other fish in the sea, Cleo,' she said aloud to the dog, who had become bored with the halt. Cleo barked, scampered off a few yards, stopped and looked back, bright-eyed.

'You're right—we should be concentrating on our walk,' she admitted, and followed the dog, turning her back on the farmhouse and the car in its courtyard.

They tramped for miles, and darkness was falling by the time they arrived back at the cottage. Physically tired out and mentally rested, Jessica lit the fire, drew the curtains against the wet night, and curled up in her chair with a book after her evening meal. Cleo dozed on the rug, and the cottage settled comfortably around them like a hen enclosing her chicks under her wings.

Ishbel arrived promptly on the following afternoon.

'All set?' she asked cheerfully when Jessica opened the door. 'Mother and David are out for the afternoon, so I thought we could have tea together afterwards. It's an ideal day for a ride—lucky we didn't arrange to go out yesterday.'

She seemed to be in high spirits. Her blue eyes sparkled, her figure was attractive and trim in a dark green sweater with cream jodhpurs. She strolled into the cottage, looking around with open interest. 'It looks nice—you've settled in, then?'

'For the time being. I'm afraid I don't have proper riding gear.'

Ishbel's eyes took in the yellow polo-necked sweater, the brown corduroy trousers and sensible shoes. 'You look fine. I've brought a hat for you, and you can bring Cleo along,' she added as the dog padded expectantly to the door. 'She often comes out with me when Adam's at the farm. She doesn't bother the horses at all.'

As she was about to step on to the path Ishbel hesitated and touched Jessica's arm tentatively. 'Look—I want to apologise for the fuss I made the other night. Of course you weren't to know where the garnets came from, I realise that.'

Her eyes were hopeful, her smile apologetic. 'Don't worry about it,' Jessica found herself saying. 'I can understand how you must have felt.'

Ishbel's smile widened. 'And thanks for sending them back—Adam's right, you didn't have any obligation to do that, and we're very grateful. He was furious with me, of course. After all,' she threw the words casually over her shoulder as she stepped out of the door, 'you're a visitor here, and it's our duty to make you feel at home while you're in Broominch.'

The horses were waiting patiently by the fence, cropping at the grass. There was Ishbel's large black horse, and a roan that seemed to Jessica to be frighteningly tall. She took a deep breath, conscious of the other girl's eyes on her.

'Manage?'

Jessica looped the reins over her arm, put her foot into the stirrup and managed, a trifle clumsily, to climb into the saddle. Ishbel busily checked the length of the stirrups for her.

'It seems a long way from the ground,' Jessica admitted. 'As I said, I haven't ridden for ages, and I was never more than a novice.'

Ishbel mounted her own horse with practised skill. 'You'll be all right. Sultan's a quiet animal.'

Once she had got used to the motion of the horse beneath her, Jessica began to relax and enjoy herself. Ishbel took her along tracks that were easy to follow, weaving in and out among trees, following a burn, passing an occasional cottage. She kept away from any difficult ground, and was careful to check with Jessica regularly. They dismounted after an hour's riding and sat on a grassy bank to give the horses a rest, then remounted and turned back in the direction of the stables.

Jessica was thoroughly enjoying herself by that time, and as they were on a wide track where they could ride side by side they were able to talk. Ishbel talked about the stables, and her hopes for the business.

'So you mean to stay here, in Broominch?'

'Of course. I've got all I want here—my family, my friends, my work. Why should I want to leave?'

'I thought you might be interested in starting your own business.'

Ishbel laughed. 'I don't need to. People who move away from home do it because they're looking for something. I've got it all here.' There was a complacent note in her voice. Then she added thoughtfully, 'The only thing I haven't got yet is Rowan Cottage. It would be such a convenient little place for me.'

Irritation tugged at Jessica's mind. 'I can understand why you want it. It's beautiful. I've enjoyed living in it.'

Ishbel turned in her saddle to look sharply at her. 'Does that mean you don't want to sell?'

'I'm not sure what I want. I've only been here for a few days, and already I know that when— if—I leave, I'll miss it very much.'

'Miss what? Broominch? Rowan Cottage? Or is it more than that?' Ishbel's voice was hard, her eyes probing.

'What more could there be?'

There was a short silence, then the other girl said, 'Jessica, I'm not a fool, even though I've spent my life in a small village. I know a little about the world. And I know about you and Adam.'

'What do you mean?'

'I know that you've been—interested in him since you first saw him. Oh, I've seen the way you look at him, the way you try to catch his attention. And I know that he spent the night with you after the dance.'

Anger flooded through Jessica. 'Just a minute, Ishbel, you have no——'

'But don't think for one moment that there's any likelihood of Adam falling in love with you. He won't. I'll see to that!' Ishbel said viciously. Then she added, her voice sweet again, 'I just thought you ought to know.'

Jessica felt her face burning. Through a haze of anger she saw a field opening before them as they emerged from a bush-lined path. The stables were among trees on the other side of the field. Her hands clenched on the reins, then loosened as she felt Sultan move restlessly.

'I expect you'd like to get back to the stables now, so we'll take a short cut,' she heard Ishbel say, and the black horse led the way into the field. Ishbel turned to look back at Jessica. 'The ground here's marshy, and a bit rough. Perhaps you'd better go round the edge and I'll meet you at the other side. It would be safer, for a novice.'

Her eyes were cool, her voice mocking. All Jessica wanted was to get back to the stables, to get away from Ishbel. She bit her lip, turned Sultan's head towards the field, ignoring his reluctance. 'I'll follow you.'

Ishbel shrugged indifferently. 'If you insist——' She clicked her tongue, and her horse moved forward confidently, picking its way between tussocks of grass. Sultan held back and Jessica, in a rush of anger that was directed at Ishbel, urged him forward sharply.

The horse surged into the field, checked abruptly, whirled around. Caught off balance, Jessica swayed in the saddle, caught at Sultan's mane, and felt the strong, rough hair slip between her fingers as she toppled forward. The ground hurried up to meet her and she knew a moment's panic as she remembered the stirrups, wondered if her feet would catch in them. Then she was lying on the ground, the sky was whirling above her, and voices fluttered about her ears.

'How was I to know she'd follow me?' That was Ishbel's voice, high-pitched and shaking. Jessica tried to move her head and found that her cheek was pressed into something tweedy, instead of grass. She blinked, and her vision cleared. She was in the field, on the ground, and her head and shoulders were being supported by a strong arm.

Faces swam into view—first Ishbel's, then Adam's, both pale and strained.

'She's coming out of it,' Ishbel said.

Jessica tried to sit up, and the sky and trees dipped and soared alarmingly.

'Just stay where you are for the moment,' Adam ordered, his arm tightening about her shoulders. A warm, wet tongue scooped at Jessica's chin, and he said irritably, 'Cleo—get back! For heaven's sake, Ishbel, I told you to hang on to that dog, didn't I?'

'Don't shout at me, Adam!' Ishbel sounded almost hysterical, but she obediently caught at the dog's collar. Jessica's vision had steadied. Beyond Ishbel's shoulder she could see the horses, both grazing calmly.

'What——' Then she remembered. She raised a hand to her aching head, but Adam captured her fingers in his own before she could touch the stinging pain above one eyebrow.

'Don't, Jessica. You cut your forehead on a stone when you went down, and it's bleeding. What about the rest of you—any bones broken?'

She moved experimentally. 'No, I'm all right. I can get up.' She struggled against him, and he helped her to her feet. The trees swooped round her again, and she was glad of his support. Ishbel's face was ashen.

'What happened?'

'You insisted on following me across the field,' Ishbel said quickly. 'Something frightened Sultan—a rabbit, perhaps—so he jumped back and you came off.'

'She should never have been riding Sultan in the first place!' Adam said angrily. 'He's far too big for someone who isn't used to riding, you know that!'

Blood mingled with the mud covering Jessica's sweater, and spotted Adam's jacket. She could feel it trickling down the side of her face. Adam mopped at her head, stuffed a crimsoned handkerchief into his pocket, and pulled a cravat from the open neck of his red shirt. He thrust it at Ishbel.

'Here—fold that into a pad,' he ordered, and she obeyed with shaking fingers. He took the pad from her and pressed it gently against Jessica's forehead. 'Hold that.'

'Head cuts bleed a lot, but it's probably just a shallow wound.'

'You'd better hope that it is, Ishbel!' Adam's voice barked over the contrite girl's, and she winced. 'Now—can you walk, Jessica, or do I carry you?'

She walked, grateful for the strength of his arm about her. It took them some time to get to the stables, Cleo staying close to Adam, Ishbel riding her black horse and leading

Sultan. In the stable yard Adam steered Jessica towards his car.

'Bring her into the house,' Ishbel protested, but he said tersely over his shoulder:

'She's going to hospital to let them have a look at that head wound.'

'I'll come with you.'

'You'd better see to your horses.' He opened the car door and helped Jessica in. As he started the engine Ishbel's lovely face, pale and drawn, appeared at the window.

'Adam, you'll come back and let me know how—how you get on?'

He sighed, nodded, and touched her hand briefly, his voice kinder. 'I'll be back, Ishbel. Just see to the horses, there's a good girl. Then make a cup of coffee for yourself and wait for me.'

As the car swung out of the yard, Jessica could see Ishbel in the rear-view mirror, a small, lonely figure staring after them until they were out of sight.

It seemed to be hours later, though it was only about seventy-five minutes, when she rejoined Adam in the waiting room of the small hospital in town. He didn't see her coming along the corridor, and she stopped outside the glass swing doors and watched him for a moment. He was out of place in the tiled, pale green room, slumped on a bench, his long legs sprawled before him. He looked tired, and that lock of hair flopped over his forehead, almost into his eyes. He stared unseeingly at a chart on the opposite wall, ignoring the other people in the room. He was in a world of his own; not, judging by the look in his eyes, a happy world. His bright red shirt and brown tweed jacket contrasted strangely with the austere room. He lifted a hand to brush the hair back from his eyes and saw her. In one movement he was on his feet, opening the door.

'Well?'

'No permanent damage.' She tried to smile up at him and felt her mouth trembling with delayed shock. 'A shallow cut on the head, a wrenched shoulder, and a slightly sprained wrist.' She nodded at the bandaged wrist. 'I must have landed on that arm, which helped to avoid a deeper cut on my head. I didn't even need stitches. I feel like a fraud.'

'You're not.' Adam guided her out of the room, his arm about her.

She leaned back in the seat as he drove her home, closing her eyes thankfully. Her head ached, her shoulder throbbed, and she looked forward to getting back to the cottage. But when the car slowed and she opened her eyes, she realised that they were turning into the driveway of the large house Adam shared with his father.

'What are we doing here?'

'You don't think I'm going to leave you on your own, do you? You can stay in my father's flat—don't worry,' he added as she began to protest, 'Mrs Kennedy won't mind staying the night to chaperone you. You won't be compromised.'

'It's a bit late to worry about that.'

Adam paused, the driver's door open. 'What does that mean?'

'It means that Ishbel saw you leaving Rowan Cottage early yesterday morning——' Jessica's voice faded and she put a hand to her head, which had begun to ache in earnest. Adam checked what he had been about to say and concentrated on helping her into the house.

Quickly, calmly, he explained matters to his father and the housekeeper. In ten minutes Jessica was in bed in the spare room and Mrs Kennedy was drawing the curtains against the evening sunshine. As she bustled out Adam appeared by the bed.

'Everything's arranged. Mrs Kennedy will stay here for tonight, and I'll take her just now to collect some night things. Then we'll go on to Rowan Cottage and she'll pack some stuff for you. Okay?'

'I'm well enough to stay at the cottage.'

'You can go back there tomorrow. Tonight you stay here,' he told her firmly. 'Just get some rest, and let me worry about everything else.' His hand closed on hers for a few seconds, strong and reassuring, then he had gone, and Jessica was drifting into a deep dreamless sleep.

She gave in to James's insistence that she should have breakfast in bed the following morning, but got up afterwards and had a hot bath before putting on the clothes Mrs Kennedy had brought back from the cottage. With the housekeeper's help, she shampooed her hair without soaking the dressing on her forehead, and by the time she joined James for lunch in the garden she was feeling like herself again.

'I'm afraid I have to go to a meeting this afternoon,' he apologised.

'I'll soak up the sun for an hour or two, then I'll get back to Rowan Cottage,' she assured him, and he lifted an eyebrow at her.

'I don't think Adam would approve.'

'I'm perfectly all right now. It was only a tumble.'

'But it could have been serious,' Adam's voice put in from behind her. He moved into her line of vision, tall and broad against the sun. 'How do you feel?'

'Fine. I thought you'd be in your office.'

'I decided to take the day off. The fall could have been serious,' he repeated.

'But it wasn't, and there's no sense in worrying over what might have been, is there?' There was a trace of annoyance in her voice, and Adam's brows came down between his eyes.

'I think that you're——' he began, then stopped as the French windows to the lawn opened and Annette Stevenson swept through them.

'We're all here,' her deep voice called as she came over to where they sat. 'The children are talking to Mrs Kennedy. My dear Jessica, how do you feel today? What a terrible thing to happen!'

Then Ishbel and David appeared, and Jessica was caught up in a wave of sympathy and concern. Ishbel, she noticed, was pale and subdued.

'I must say, if I had a pound for every time I've taken a fall I'd be a rich woman now,' Annette swept on.

'You already are a rich woman, Annette,' James Brodie put in dryly.

'Nonsense, James, I'm a businesswoman trying to make ends meet. And unless I get your support at that conservation meeting, I'm not going to have any decent rides left for my pupils. You are coming, I hope? Good—I'll take you in my car.' She hurried on, a born organiser. 'Now—Ishbel has to go into town to look at some riding tack I want; since you're here, Adam, you wouldn't mind driving her there, would you?'

'Would you, darling?' Ishbel linked her hand through his arm. 'That would be marvellous. Otherwise I'll have to go back to the farmhouse and collect the Land Rover.'

Adam hesitated, glancing at Jessica.

'I don't expect Jessica will mind,' Ishbel put in swiftly. 'After all, she seems to have got over the fall, and David can keep her company.'

'My pleasure,' David smiled down at Jessica. 'It'll give us a chance to talk.'

Adam looked from one to the other, frowning. 'Jessica——'

She smiled brightly at him. 'I'd enjoy an afternoon with David,' she lied.

His eyes darkened, but he only said, 'In that case, I'm free to take you into town, Ishbel.'

As she watched them go, Ishbel's arm looped round Adam's waist, his hand on her shoulder,

Jessica found herself envying the other girl. She would always regret that she hadn't met Adam Brodie under other circumstances, in another place.

'Hey—remember me?' David's voice cut across her thoughts and she turned towards him, smiling.

'Sorry—I was lost in a dream.'

His blue eyes flicked from hers to the windows that had just closed behind the others, then back to Jessica. 'What does he have that I haven't?' he wondered aloud, mournfully.

'Who?'

'Don't try to pull the wool over my eyes, my love. Adam, that's who. Ishbel pines for him, and now you've got that broody look in your eyes.'

'That's mild concussion!'

'No—broodiness. Perhaps it's because he's the strong silent type. Women always want what they can't get.'

'Except Ishbel.'

'A trace of cattiness there? Ishbel usually gets what she wants, that's true, but I'm beginning to wonder if she's met her match in Adam. You should have heard him last night!'

'Last night?'

'After your fall. He came back to the farm quite late, and poor Ishbel heard a few home truths. I don't know what upset her most,' David said thoughtfully, 'being shouted at by Adam, or having her ability as a riding instructor questioned.'

'There's nothing wrong with her ability. I just couldn't handle the horse, that's all. I fell off, like a nervous beginner.'

He rolled on to his stomach on the grass and eyed her thoughtfully. 'That what you think? Darling, Sultan's a steady animal—no tricks, no hassle usually. But you came off in that rough, marshy field near the stables, didn't you? He was frightened by a rabbit in that field, when he was younger. He hates it. We have to let him skirt it—or he gets difficult. No problem even with a new rider on his back, as long as he goes round the edge of the place. But you made him go across it, apparently.'

In the pause that followed, Jessica could feel his bright blue eyes studying her face. She gave her attention to a button on her dress, twisting it between her fingers.

'Ishbel claims that you insisted on taking Sultan across that field,' David said softly. 'But I think she let you cross it without warning you of the consequences. Right?'

'Why should she do that?'

'Oh—jealously. She wanted you to take a tumble in the mud, and make a fool of yourself.'

'Don't be silly, David, what reason does she have to be jealous of me?' But in Jessica's mind's eye, as she spoke, was a picture of Adam leaving the cottage, Ishbel riding past the gate a few minutes later. She recalled the girl's voice saying 'I know that he spent the night with you.'

'Now you sound like a schoolmarm,' David said impishly. 'You don't know Ishbel—she used to play some very mean tricks on me when we were kids. I think she played one on you—though she didn't mean you to hit your head on a stone. She got a bad fright when she thought you were badly hurt. And I think that Adam has a suspicion that Ishbel's not as innocent as she makes out about the whole thing.'

Jessica's mouth was dry, but she spoke clearly and firmly. 'You're both wrong. Ishbel did warn me that I should go round the edge of the field, and I insisted that I could handle the horse. So, you see, the fall was my fault—my fault entirely!'

Was it her imagination, or was there a trace of disappointment in David's blue gaze? He shrugged, turned the conversation to other topics, and was an entertaining, interesting companion for the rest of the afternoon. The small drama of the dance melted into the past, and was forgotten, Jessica was pleased to note.

But his revelation about Sultan's dislike of the marshy field had painted another black cloud on the horizon for Jessica. As she talked to David, part of her mind was going over the moments before her fall.

Ishbel had warned her, partly, about crossing the field on Sultan. But her warning had been shaped in such a way that Jessica had been pushed into defying it. She had certainly said nothing about Sultan's dislike of the place.

David was right. Ishbel had hoped to see

Jessica make a fool of herself. Ishbel was a lovely, spoiled child who disliked being challenged over the ownership of the cottage—or over Adam Brodie.

She was a bad enemy. Although the sun was warm on the garden, Jessica shivered, with the feeling that someone had just walked over her grave.

CHAPTER NINE

'COME up and see my flat,' Adam invited Jessica when he met her going into the house later. 'My father called to say he's staying at the Stevensons' place for a meal. They invited us, but I turned it down. I thought you'd rather not.'

'I was just about to leave for the cottage.'

'I'll drive you back later. I was going to take the opportunity to give you dinner in my flat. It's all right, I can cook,' he added with a slight smile. 'I'm not going to ask you to make it. All right, Mrs Kennedy?' he asked as the housekeeper came from the kitchen.

'Certainly. In fact, if you're going to eat upstairs, perhaps I can get home.'

He smiled down at her with genuine affection. 'Good grief, you've been stuck here since last night—we all forgot about that! I'll drive you home now.' He swept her protests aside. 'Jessica won't mind waiting for ten minutes, will you, Jessica? Won't be long.' And he escorted the housekeeper out.

While she waited for him to get back, Jessica dried the plates on the draining-board in the large kitchen, then brushed her hair into a shining cap and added a touch of colour to her lips. Her shoulder was still stiff and her wrist felt weak, but otherwise she was back to normal. She examined her face in a mirror and decided that apart from the large piece of lint and sticking plaster on her forehead she was presentable.

Adam carried a bottle of wine when he returned. He smiled at Jessica, in a relaxed mood. 'I thought we'd dine in style. I enjoy cooking for other people. We could use the inside staircase, but you might as well see the changes I made, so we'll use my official door.'

When they went outside the sky was dull and the air was hushed, as though waiting for something to happen. From a distance, as they went round the corner of the house, came the low rumble of thunder.

Adam's flat was reached by an enclosed staircase at the side of the house, by the garage. A door at the top opened right into a large sitting-room furnished in shades of brown and gold. It was a comfortable room, with large chairs, and walls covered with book-shelves and pictures. The big windows gave a sweeping view of the valley, rising in the distance to soft, rolling hills.

The dogs came hurrying to meet her when Adam opened the kitchen door in the far wall, and he called them back sternly. Toby cringed, tail between his legs, and licked meekly at her hand. Cleo gave her the more relaxed greeting of an old friend, then the dogs settled before the log-effect gas fire. The room was getting dark, and Adam switched on a few lamps.

'A storm's coming up.' He looked out of the window. 'It rolls round the hills here for hours at a time. I think we'll see this one before the evening's out, though.'

'Can I help?'

'You could set the table.' He led the way into a large, well-equipped kitchen, taking off his brown safari jacket and hanging it on the back of the door. 'This used to be a bedroom, and I've got a bathroom, study and my own bedroom. You'll find cutlery and mats in that cupboard. Just hunt around.'

'It seems a shame to split a fine old house in two.'

Adam was bent over the kitchen table, and she couldn't see his face. His fingers didn't cease in their work. 'I doubt if I'd ever want the entire house anyway. One flat is ample for me. It could be changed back into one big house if necessary—if any future owners wanted it like that.'

Lightning was flickering along the dark grey horizon as Jessica set the table, which was in the big bay window of the sitting-room. She began to draw the curtains, then decided against it, and left them open.

Adam, completely absorbed in his cooking, shooed her out of the kitchen when she tried to help, so she curled up in an armchair with a book from the shelves. She could hear him moving about, could hear dishes clattering and, eventually, came the sizzle of hot fat and the smell of meat cooking. The dogs lifted their muzzles and sniffed appreciatively. By the time Adam called her to the table, Jessica was hungry.

'Dinner is served.' He bowed her to her chair with exaggerated courtesy, and poured wine into long-stemmed glasses. A pale pink rose, just unfurling from the tight bud, lay by her plate.

'Just thought I'd give you a stylish evening,' he said when she picked it up.

The meal was beautifully cooked, and beautifully served. When she looked surprised, he flushed slightly and told her, 'I live on my own, you know. And I was away from home for a few years. I had to learn to cook to survive. Now I cook because I enjoy it.'

She wondered, as he refilled her glass, how often he had cooked dinner for Ishbel, how often the two of them had sat, as she and Adam were sitting now, facing each other across the polished table, glasses and silver glittering in the lamplight, the gracious room providing a perfect backdrop to Ishbel's dark beauty. How often, she wondered as she became aware of the delicate scent from the rose pinned to her dress, had he given a rose to Ishbel? Deep red roses, of course, to complement her lush colouring——

'You don't like the sweet?' he asked gently, and she blinked. 'Oh—yes, I do. I was just thinking about something.'

They washed the dishes, at Jessica's insistence, then made coffee. The dogs had eaten in the kitchen, and Adam took them to their kennels in the garden while Jessica carried the tray of coffee to the small fireside table. When he got back she was curled up on a chair.

'It was a really lovely meal, Adam,' she smiled

up at him. 'Thank you for inviting me.'

'I felt that it was the least I could do.' He sat down opposite her. 'You've been having a rough time recently.'

'Didn't you have something else fixed up for this evening?'

'Nothing—important.' His voice was smooth, his eyes hooded. 'Nothing that couldn't be put off until some other time. Would you like some brandy, or a liqueur?'

She chose *crème de menthe*, and he poured brandy into a balloon glass for himself. He put a record on the stereo, then sat opposite her.

'I meant to ask you——' Jessica broke the silence. 'Ishbel's grandfather was called Edward, wasn't he?'

'Yes, he was. Why do you ask?'

She explained about the inscription on the book at Rowan Cottage. 'Now I have something that was special for Kate. I have the book.'

He smiled faintly. 'I thought you were shocked at Kate's affair.'

'Just—surprised, at first. It didn't seem to be the sort of life she would lead. I never thought of her as a romantic person.'

'She was an incurable romantic, as it happens.' He stared into the depths of his brandy glass. 'She once told me that I should stop listening with my ears, and start listening with my heart.'

'And did you?'

'Of course not—it isn't possible.' His voice was brisk.

'Perhaps you're afraid of being hurt,' she dared to say.

He was silent for so long that she thought he had taken offence, then he said, 'Perhaps. Is that so terrible?'

'Have you ever been hurt?'

His eyes were guarded again. 'I learned a long time ago that he who puts his hand into the fire stands a good chance of being burned. I never allow myself to be burned.'

'Everyone has to take chances, sooner or later.'

'That's a sweeping statement!'

'It's true. The more I hear about Kate Ogilvie, the more I feel sure that she was right. She knew what she wanted, and she was prepared to pay the price,' Jessica said firmly.

He shook his dark head. 'I was very fond of her. I'm glad I knew her. But she could have done so much with her life. Instead, she buried herself in Broominch and let the world go by. It was such a waste!'

'She loved, and she was loved!'

Thunder rolled around the house, encircling them with its low muttering. Here, in the comfortable, lamp-lit room, they were protected from the storm outside.

Adam raised an eyebrow. 'So you think that Kate did the right thing?'

She tilted her chin, faced him. 'Not entirely. In her place, I'd have married the man I loved, and be damned to any old principles!'

He stared, and then laughed, a sound of pure amusement. 'I believe you would, at that!

Love comes first, eh?'
· 'I think so.'
'And what about the reality of life, after the
first glow is over?' There was a harsh note in his
voice now, and the amusement had disappeared
from his brown eyes as they caught and held her
gaze. 'What about the disillusionment, the pain of
finding out that it was all a mistake? You'd want
to go through that, for the sake of a few days—
weeks—of happiness? Life isn't a fairy-tale,
Jessica!'
'I know that. If I was sure, if I was really in
love, then there wouldn't be disillusionment.
There would be ups and downs, rough patches,
and perhaps unhappiness from time to time. But
that's life. I'd still love him, and if we were right
for each other, he'd still love me, no matter what
tried to come between us.'
'Easy enough to say now,' he challenged. 'But
have you ever been in that situation? Have you
ever met a man who isn't meant for you, but a
man you love anyway—completely, deeply. Has
that ever happened, Jessica?'
'I——' she stopped, the words dying in her
throat. A few days earlier she would have
admitted freely that her picture of love was only
imagination. But now, with Adam sitting opposite, his eyes holding hers, her voice deserted
her. He belonged in Broominch, and she didn't.
He belonged to Ishbel, and Jessica had no right
to feel as she did about him. The silence
deepened as they stared at each other, and it was
Adam himself who broke it, raising his glass.

'Perhaps that wasn't a fair question,' he said with a laugh, though his eyes, still fixed on her face, were serious. 'Perhaps it's better if we just agree to differ, and drink a toast to Kate and her Edward.'

Jessica lifted her glass, and was surprised to find that her hand was steady. As they drank, thunder boomed out almost above their heads and they both glanced instinctively at the ceiling.

'That was close.'

'What about the dogs?'

'They're fine in the kennels.' Adam moved to the window to draw the curtains, then stopped, his hand held out to her. 'Come and look—or are you afraid of storms?'

'Not at all.' She followed him as he put out the standard lamp beside the table. The window gave them a grandstand view as flashes of lightning threw every detail of the valley into sharp relief. Then the pane before them was black, and thunder rolled before the window glowed briefly with a blue-white glare of lightning again.

Jessica moved in front of Adam, and stood watching the storm, spell-bound. 'Fantastic, isn't it?' he murmured into her ear. They watched for a long time before she drew a deep breath and turned to him. 'Adam, I should probably get back to the cottage before the rain starts.'

'Okay.' He took the empty glass from her fingers and put it on the table. A flash of lightning held the two of them in its embrace for a second, and Jessica was left with a vivid picture of Adam standing over her, every line of his face etched into her mind, and into her heart.

She began to push past him, panic-stricken, intent on getting away before her longing for him let her down. But he caught at her arm, and before she knew what was happening she was in his arms, her hungry body pressed against his, her hands reaching up to touch his hair, his face, the warm strength of his shoulders beneath his thin shirt.

The memory of that first time in his arms hadn't played her false. His touch was as thrilling as it had been then, his lips as possessive, his passion as strong. Outside, the thunder and lightning continued to dominate the countryside, but Adam and Jessica ignored it, caught up as they were in their immediate need for each other. The fire that had warmed her before blazed up under his touch, and consumed her body.

Her hands found their way beneath his shirt, caressed his smooth skin, and in answer he whispered, 'My darling——' before claiming her mouth yet again with his kisses.

She could feel him trembling, could sense his desire to take her warring with a reluctance to commit either of them further. But the joy she felt in his embrace threw her own caution to the winds.

'Adam——' He drew back and looked down at

her, his eyes dazed. Jessica took a deep breath.
'Adam, I——'

The doorbell, soft and melodious as it was,
jolted them apart as though it had been a fire
alarm. They stared at each other.

'Oh—hell! I'd better see who it is,' he muttered,
running his fingers through his hair. Then he had
gone, and the precious delicate thread between
them was broken. Jessica found herself hurrying to
switch on the lamp, smoothing her hair and
fastening the top button of her dress with trembling
fingers. She remembered the heat of his lips against
her shoulder as though it had happened to someone
else, or in a dream which would never return.

The dream faded to a faint, faraway memory as
voices echoed on the stairs, and Jessica recognised
Ishbel Stevenson's clear, crisp tones.

Adam came in first, glancing quickly round the
room. Jessica, sitting in an armchair with a book
on her lap, noticed that he had found time to
smooth his hair back and tuck his shirt in on his
way to the door.

'A surprise visitor,' he said calmly. 'Want some
coffee, Ishbel? I was just going to take Jessica
home.'

'In that case, I won't bother with the coffee.'
Ishbel came forward to the fire and turned up the
heater with the ease of one who was at home in
the room. She wore a crimson plastic raincoat
and hood, and her eyes were as bright as the wet
plastic. 'I didn't expect to see you here, Jessica.'

'I couldn't let her go without giving her a
sample of my excellent cooking.'

'I suppose not.' Ishbel's voice was as brittle as the smile she bestowed on them both. 'He's a very good cook, isn't he? I'll save you a journey, Adam. I brought Uncle James home, and I can take Jessica back to the cottage—if that's what she wants.'

'I'll take her back,' Adam said firmly. 'I'm taking Cleo as well, and she won't travel in your car.'

Ishbel's eyes flashed from one face to the other, and two red spots began to glow in her cheeks. Then she announced triumphantly, 'Then I'll wait here for you. You won't be long, will you, darling?'

He looked at his watch. 'My God, Ishbel, do you know what time it is? I've to be at the office tomorrow morning——'

'It isn't that late, and I have something important to discuss with you. Besides——' she reached up from where she sat on the rug, and took his hand in hers, 'I've known you to stay up until the small hours without complaining. Don't tell me you're getting too old—or too dull!'

He surveyed her with mingled exasperation and anger. 'Oh—very well, if that's what you want. Ready, Jessica?'

Pleased with her success, Ishbel rose smoothly to her feet. 'And I'll make fresh coffee while you're away. You'll be back by the time it's ready,' she added pointedly, slipping out of the mackintosh. Beneath it she wore a plain dress in pale yellow. It emphasised her figure and her dark loveliness, and fitted very well with the room she stood in. 'Better put something over your head, Jessica. It's pouring outside.'

'Here,' Adam brought a raincoat together with his jacket. 'Put that over your head.' He donned his jacket and an anorak, and picked up his keys from a shelf. 'Ready?'

'Oh——' Ishbel, on her way to the table with an empty coffee cup, stooped to the carpet. 'What a pity—look!'

In the outstretched palm was a pale pink rose, newly opened but crushed and battered. Jessica stared dumbly at it, forcing her hands to stay by her sides, checking the instinctive gesture towards her shoulder, where the rose had been pinned. It must have been pulled free while she was in Adam's arms, must have fallen to the floor and been trampled underfoot in those blind, mad moments when all that mattered was being close to him, touching him.

'And it was such a lovely rose, too,' Ishbel's voice tinkled on, a crystal goblet filled to the brim with pure venom. The bright spots in her cheeks glowed. Adam crossed to her in two long strides, took the flower from her fingers, and tossed it carelessly into the waste-paper basket.

'It really doesn't matter,' he said casually. 'Coming, Jessica?'

She followed him down the stairs and out into the rainy night. The thunder was retreating now, the lightning moving further into the darkness. The rain held sway. Jessica let Adam settle her in the passenger seat of the car and accepted Cleo's moist kisses as the dog jumped into the back seat.

During the short drive back to Rowan Cottage
he concentrated on the road, which could be
glimpsed as a river through each clear swathe of
glass left by the busy windscreen wipers. Jessica
huddled beside him, lost in her own thoughts.

When they reached the cottage she fumbled
with the key before getting the door open. With
the lights on, the cottage instantly became the
friendly haven she had grown to love. She drew
the curtains, and took off the raincoat as Adam
brought Cleo's food and blanket in.

'I set the fire earlier today,' he threw over his
shoulder as he went into the kitchen with his
burden. 'And I brought in some food.'

She knelt on the rug and struck a match. The
small flame caught paper and lighters, and grew.
Carefully arranged sticks caught, crackled, began
to throw out a faint warmth.

'I think that's everything,' he said from behind
her. She got to her feet and picked up the coat.
He took it.

'I'm sorry, Jessica. Sorry the evening was
spoiled, and that——'

'My fault. You're right, I'm an incurable
romantic. And a bit stupid as well.' She
swallowed hard. 'I keep making things difficult
for you, but I don't really set out to, though you
won't believe that.'

'What on earth are you talking about?' he asked
from above her bent head. She blundered on.

'About me—I'm not in the habit of throwing
myself at men the way I——'

'What?'

'Perhaps it's because I'm Kate Ogilvie's great-niece.'

He put his hands on her shoulders, and shook her hard. 'That's enough, Jessica! Now listen to me, young lady—Kate Ogilvie was special, I've told you that more than once. And I'm not going to let you run her down, or yourself either. Do you understand me?'

She looked up at him, too distraught to see the expression in his eyes. 'But you must see for yourself what a mess I'm making of everything—what I'm doing to you and to Ishbel, and to David!'

'You?' His laugh was a bleak sound. 'My dear child, you're too naïve to harm anyone except yourself. For heaven's sake, you didn't force David to go over the score the other night. And you've never had to act the temptress with me either, surely you know that! I'm the one who's at fault—me, and nobody else! And now I'm going before I say or do the wrong thing again!'

She touched his arm as he made for the hall. 'Adam, I don't——'

He swung round, his face filled with dark shadows. He caught her in his arms and kissed her once, a crushing, bruising kiss that was over before she realised that it was happening. When he let her go she put a hand to the doorway to steady herself.

'Don't expect me to sit down and discuss anything, Jessica,' he said harshly. 'Just believe me when I say that nothing can come of it. It was wrong from the beginning!' Then he plunged through the rain that glittered in the light like strips of cellophane, and disappeared into the night.

'Adam!' When there was no answer to her call, Jessica ran out of the door and down the path, slipping on wet flagstones, splashing through puddles. She fumbled with the gate, which was slick with water. Rain blinded her and plastered her thin dress against her body.

Adam's car roared into life, and as she stumbled forward through the gate the vehicle pulled away. Through streaming glass she could see Adam's face, pale and set, turned away from her. Then the car had gone, and she was alone in the roadway, the rain driving wet hair into her eyes.

Cleo's nose was pushed gently, insistently, into her hand. The dog whined for attention, and Jessica led her back into Rowan Cottage, shutting the door against the storm.

David arrived shortly after Jessica got up the next day. She stared when she saw him on the doorstep, acutely aware that she was wearing a shabby sweater and her old jeans, and that her face was free of make-up.

'I met the postman,' he said cheerfully, 'and I thought this might be the excuse I need to beg a cup of coffee.'

She took the envelope from him. 'My first letter! That calls for coffee—I could even manage a boiled egg if you want one.'

They ate in the kitchen, perched on stools. Then David helped her to wash up and volunteered to bring in more firewood from the shed.

'It looks as though the weather's broken,' he squinted up at the grey sky. 'But you didn't do too badly for sunshine here—we don't get much of it.'

From the kitchen window she could see him carrying armfuls of wood from the shed. Her mistrust of him had gone completely, and she found something very likeable in this tall, easy-going young man with the lovely eyes. If only he could stir her blood the way Adam could, but there was no sense in such day-dreaming, she told herself sternly.

'I wish we'd met somewhere else,' David said unexpectedly, echoing her own thoughts when he had filled the log basket.

She blinked at him, taken aback. 'I don't know what you're talking about!' But she felt colour rising into her face.

'You're thinking along the same lines,' he said shrewdly, grinning down at her. 'Admit it. If only you'd met me when I wasn't at home. I usually show my serious side when I'm away from Broominch. If only I hadn't behaved like an idiot the other night. You wouldn't like to give me a second chance, would you?'

'At what?' she asked warily, and he laughed.

'At getting to know me. Let's take off for the day, just you and me.'

She would have accepted at any other time. But she was still suffering from the after-effects of the previous evening, still haunted by Adam's kisses, his sudden, bewildering anger. She couldn't stop wondering how long Ishbel had stayed with him, in that cosy flat with the storm lashing outside.

'I've already made plans for today,' she said firmly. 'There's a friend of the family near here, and I promised to go and visit her.'

If he sensed that she was lying he gave no sign of it. 'Come back in time for dinner. Please?' His eyes were serious, almost pleading.

'If you'll do me a favour and take Cleo for the day. I don't want to take her, and I can't leave her on her own all day.'

David waited while she changed into a pale brown trouser suit with a deep brown shirt, and they left together. 'I can only hope that that outfit isn't going to be wasted on a friend of your parents',' he said solemnly, his blue eyes travelling over her with open admiration. 'Don't forget your letter, you haven't opened it yet.'

She slipped the airmail letter into her bag, locked the cottage door, and got into the car. Cleo whined softly, tugging at the lead David held, but quietened when he patted her and told her, 'Okay, old girl, we're keeping each other company until she gets back.'

Jessica waved, and turned the car away from the village. David and Cleo stood together outside the cottage gate, watching her until the car disappeared. There was something lonely about man and dog, and for a moment she regretted the lie about a family friend. But she needed time to herself, to recapture the confident, sensible Jessica Taylor who had first arrived in Broominch.

She drove for miles, found a small market town where she shopped, and in a sudden burst of extravagance bought a pale pink dress, the colour of the rose Adam had given her the night before. The dress was sleeveless, with a deep neckline and flared, soft skirt.

The afternoon was spent exploring a small castle that, with its grounds, was open to the public. She bought a handful of postcards and settled in the castle tea-room, a converted dungeon, to write 'wish you were here' cards. For the first time she began to think of the school, her flat, her friends. She realised, sadly, that it was time to go back to her normal routine, time to put the summer behind her.

The past week or two had been stormy, exciting—and painful. But it was all unreal. None of it could ever be real, for her. Not even Adam, with his strange moods and his sudden passion.

She sighed for what might have been. Slipping the finished cards into her bag, she found the letter David had handed her, and opened it. For a long time she sat there, reading and re-reading it. Then she put it away, and stared unseeingly at the stone walls of the room. A slight smile touched her lips.

Perhaps she was forced to admit defeat; but Ishbel Stevenson wouldn't get everything her own way, after all.

CHAPTER TEN

THE rose-coloured dress set off Jessica's grey
eyes and fair hair to perfection. With it she wore
the rope of pearls that had belonged to Kate
Ogilvie. After some hesitation, she slipped the
friendship ring, with its seed pearls and its
plaited hair, on to her finger.

'You're beautiful,' David said simply as they
sat in a small restaurant in the town, by the old
bridge. Below the window where they ate the
river flowed by, reflecting the lamps that were set
on the bridge. Night added a magic touch to the
water.

'I'm very ordinary.'

He shook his head. 'No, you're beautiful, you
just don't realise it. You even make me wish that
I was ready to settle down—but I'm not, more's
the pity. And by the time I am, you'll probably
be married to some lucky man.'

'I think I'm going to be a career woman.' She
lifted her glass and sipped at the red wine.

'Not you. Ishbel's a career woman, but you
aren't ruthless enough. You're more feminine
than she is, and that's why she's jealous.'

'That's nonsense!'

'Oh, Jessica——' his voice was exasperated.
'Come on, darling, you're with me, remember?

No need to pretend. It's obvious that Ishbel's jealous because Adam's crazy about you.'

'He's what?' She stared across the table at him.

'You should have heard him after I made a pass at you, and again after you came off Sultan. I've never known Adam to make such a fuss over a client's well-being before. Don't try to tell me that it's just a business relationship. You've noticed that you have a strange effect on the man, surely?'

'I've—I've noticed that he's a difficult person to know.'

David surveyed her with amused blue eyes. ' "Difficult" isn't exactly the word I'd use for him lately. He usually keeps his real feelings well under lock and key. Come to think of it, that describes Adam perfectly. It's as though his real self is locked safely away. But over the past few days—well, he's been different. More fire to him. Blood will out, they say. We're a bad lot, we Brodies—or didn't you know about that? I always thought old Adam had missed it, but I'm beginning to wonder.'

'But you're not a Brodie, David.'

'Oh yes, I am. At least, Mum is.'

'But—you mean that your grandfather was——'

'Old Edward Brodie. Uncle James's cousin. Mind you, I don't reckon old Edward was that wild. He just married the wrong woman in his hot-blooded youth, before your great-aunt came along. If he'd married her, we'd be related, I suppose——'

His voice flowed on, but Jessica had stopped listening. Now she knew why Adam had drawn back after taking her in his arms, why he had shouted at her 'I'm the one who's at fault!' James, Edward, David—the wild, womanising Brodies lived on. And all his life, determined not to hurt a woman as his father had hurt his mother, Adam had fought against his own blood. Now she knew why, from time to time, she had glimpsed a harsher, more stormy, exciting man beneath Adam's quiet, indifferent mask.

But it wouldn't make any difference, she realised almost at once. She couldn't break down the wall he had built around himself. She would still have to go away from him.

'Hey,' David said gently, 'are you still with me?'

She looked up, forced a smile to her lips. 'Where else would I be?'

'Family histories are boring, I know. Let's change the subject,' said David, and did so.

They strolled across the old bridge afterwards, back to the car-park. Then they drove to the farm, where Jessica was to collect Cleo.

'Surprise, surprise—Adam's here.' David said casually as he opened the door. She felt her heart flip over, and dug her nails into the palms of her hands as she followed him into the house.

In the large hall, he took her coat. 'Go on in, love, while I hang this up.'

The living-room was lovely in lamplight, a sprawling room that was almost shabby, but designed entirely for comfort.

The air outside was cool enough for a log fire to be burning in the large hearth. Adam stood before it, listening to Ishbel, who was sitting on a deep sofa with her back to the door. A lamp threw its glow on to his face and Jessica hesitated in the shadows by the door, her eyes taking in the thick, tumbled hair, the strong mouth and well-shaped face before she moved forward.

He looked up and saw her standing on the fringe of the pool of light, the rose-coloured dress and pearl necklace softly lit, her throat rising from the dress like a slender stem. Adam stared, and then gathered himself together and said evenly, 'Hullo, Jessica.'

Ishbel rose from the sofa, beautiful in a white full-sleeved blouse and dark green trousers, her hands outstretched in welcome. 'Jessica, how nice! Have you come to collect Cleo?'

'She's come for a nightcap,' David said breezily, steering Jessica to a seat with one arm around her shoulers.

'Telling Adam all about the course you're going on, Ishbel?' he went on, as he poured a small glass of sherry for Jessica.

'I still think it's the wrong time for me to go away,' Ishbel said sulkily, and Adam shot an irritated glance at her. Obviously they had been arguing.

'I told you, Ishbel—if your mother has decided that this is the right time to expand the business, then I bow to her experience.'

'But Adam——' she reached out a hand and placed it on his arm, but he turned back to the fire, and her fingers fell to her side.

'There's nothing more to be said, Ishbel. Talk to your mother about it, not me. Besides, Jessica doesn't want to listen to all this. It's boring, for a stranger.'

Jessica stared down into the amber liquid in her glass. 'Surely I'm not a stranger.' She looked up, and smiled sweetly at Adam. 'At least, I hope not.'

Ishbel looked at her sharply. 'Does that mean you're going to stay in Broominch?'

Jessica savoured the moment, aware that she had their full attention. 'Not exactly. I got a letter from my parents today. It seems that there's a possibility that my father will be transferred to his firm's Scottish office. My parents are coming home for a holiday in September, and they want to see Rowan Cottage. They might be interested in buying it from me.'

Ishbel's gasp broke the silence. Her face was a mask of fury. 'But you promised to sell the cottage to me!'

'She didn't,' Adam spoke before Jessica could. 'You wanted first refusal, but Jessica never promised anything, Ishbel.' His face was expressionless as he surveyed Jessica. 'Obviously she must think of her family first.'

'Absolutely,' David agreed. 'We're not family are we, Ishbel? In fact, Jessica's had a rough time with us, one way and another. I expect she'd be very happy to sell the cottage to her parents.'

'Jessica—you can't!'

She shrugged, meeting Ishbel's angry gaze

levelly. 'I have to let them see the place. I can hardly make any decisions until they've been here. Besides,' now she looked at Adam, 'I like my parents. They're happy people, and Rowan Cottage needs happy owners.' She lifted her glass, her eyes still holding his. 'To Kate and Edward,' she toasted, and drank.

A faint smile curved the corners of his mouth. 'To Kate and Edward,' he agreed in a low voice.

Ishbel looked suspiciously from Adam to Jessica. 'What's that supposed to mean?' she began, but David's voice drowned her out.

'So you'll be here for the rest of the summer, Jessica? If you are——'

She put the glass down and rose to her feet. 'No, I think it's time I went home.' As Adam opened his mouth to say something she turned away from him. 'Can I have my coat, David?'

As he went to get it, Ishbel stormed across the room, then swung round, her face tight with anger. 'I think it's ridiculous. Adam, tell her that I have first refusal—it's on our land, and I——'

'Be quiet, Ishbel,' he said, without raising his voice, and she stopped, her eyes wide with shock. David came back with the coat.

'I'll walk down the lane with you.'

'I'd rather just take Cleo and go back alone,' she told him steadily, and he hesitated, then shrugged.

'All right, Jess—whatever you want.'

Cleo got up from the rug when Jessica called her name, then turned towards Adam, confused. He touched her head with one large, capable hand. 'Go with Jessica, girl,' he told her, and she followed Jessica across the room.

Jessica was almost at the front door when she heard Adam call her name. She reached the door, opened it. Behind her she could hear Ishbel calling 'Adam! For heaven's sake——' and David's amused 'I think you've just met your Waterloo, little sister.' Then the door closed behind her, and she and Cleo were outside.

The front door opened and slammed shut. Footsteps tapped sharply on the flagstones at her back. 'Get into the car,' Adam said shortly. 'I'll drive you home.'

She kept on walking. 'No, thank you.'

'Jessica—get into that car!' There was an edge to his voice. 'I want to talk to you!'

'If it's about maintenance of the cottage, I'll come into your office tomorrow.'

'Jessica!'

She stopped, whirled round to look up at him. 'I want to walk home!'

'Right!' he said between his teeth, then she was almost lifted off her feet as he caught at her arm with one firm hand and set off down the lane at a rapid pace, dragging her along with him.

'Adam! What—what on earth are you doing?' She tried to pull free, but his fingers were like steel clamps.

'You wanted to walk home—well, I'm walking you home!' he said firmly. In the darkness, she couldn't see what lay in her path, and with Adam dragging her along, she had no time to step carefully. She tripped and stumbled, squeaked as she splashed through a puddle, then almost fell, and was lifted and dragged on by his grip on her arm.

'You don't have to be so—oh, Adam, my shoe—I've lost my shoe—Adam!' she almost screamed at him, but he continued his headlong march down the long, dark lane, and she had no option but to go with him.

'I'll find it in the morning. I'll buy you more shoes,' he said breathlessly. She tried to hold back, but the speed he was moving at made it impossible for her to do any more than run to keep up, in case she lost her footing and was dragged through the mud. Then she stepped on a stone with her stockinged foot and cried out. Without stopping, Adam swept her up in his arms and continued down the lane.

'Adam Brodie, will you—this is ridiculous!' she raved against his shoulder. 'This is like—do you know what you're like? The old Brodies, that's what! The Border raiders—the woman stealers!'

'And I should have admitted to being one of them long ago,' Adam said briskly. A car passed as he swung her into the road, and Jessica glimpsed a pale, surprised face at the window before the vehicle disappeared along the road. He managed, somehow, to open the garden gate, and marched up the path.

'Key!' he ordered, and she found herself fumbling in her bag for the key, then opening the door. He walked into the hall and kicked the front door shut behind him. Cleo, who had run ahead into the cottage, seemed quite unmoved by the entire episode.

'Lights!'

She found the light switch and the room was lit.

'Adam Brodie, put me down at once!'

'Certainly.' He walked over to an armchair and dropped her on to it as though she was a sack of coal. Then he drew the curtains and poked the fire into a blaze, whistling softly to himself while Jessica got her breath back.

'Look at me—just look at me! Her voice shook with rage. Adam dropped into the opposite chair and sprawled there, at ease. His brown eyes took their time travelling over her.

'I think you look wonderful.'

'My stockings—and my shoe's missing, and look at the mud on my dress, and——' she felt tears coming to her eyes and scrubbed them away with the back of her hand. 'What do you think you're doing?'

'Coming to my senses,' he said cheerfully. 'I'll buy you a new dress, and new shoes, and stockings—I owe you a pair of stockings already, don't I? I didn't realise that abducting women was such an enjoyable pastime, I must admit. No wonder my ancestors preferred it to cattle rustling. I should have given in to the Brodie blood the first time I saw you.'

'Adam.' She tried to get the schoolteacher note in her voice. 'Adam, please get up and go away—now. And never come back.'

He shook his head slowly, brows drawn down

in a thoughtful frown over bright eyes. In his open-necked tawny-coloured shirt, which high-lighted the gold lights in his eyes and his hair, he looked like an adventurer. 'No—I don't think the Brodies would get out and stay out once they'd abducted their women. I think they probably kissed them.'

He had plucked her out of her chair and into his arms before she had a chance to protest. Her coat fell to the floor, and her arms, after weakly trying to push him away, crept round his neck and held him close.

'Then,' Adam said thoughtfully when he had lifted his head from hers, 'I think they probably kissed them again.'

This time he kissed her tenderly, deeply, and with a longing that left them both breathless.

'And after that——' Adam continued, holding her within the circle of his arms, close enough for her to feel his heart pounding through the thin material of his shirt. 'After that, they might have had the sense to say, please don't ever go away, my darling, darling Jessica. Because if you do, my life won't make sense any more.'

'But——' He stopped her words with a passionate kiss, then let his lips travel lightly over her face.

'I love you, Jessica. I've loved you since the evenings when I sat here and listened to Kate talking about you. I wanted to see you, talk to you—and when you finally arrived, I was so afraid of hurting you that I almost lost you. I couldn't bear to think of you suffering like the other women who were foolish enough to fall in love with a Brodie.'

'Couldn't I make up my own mind about that?' she asked, and felt the laughter rising in his chest.

'That's what I didn't anticipate—that you'd have a strong mind of your own, my darling'

'Oh, Adam, you've been such a fool!'

He lifted her face to his, smoothed her hair back, and kissed her gently. 'I know that. Remember my telling you that Kate said I should listen with my heart? I started, this evening. And all I could hear was you, Jessica.'

She reached up to entangle her fingers in his hair. 'You heard me before—but you just wouldn't admit it!'

He kissed her again, then wondered when they finally drew apart, 'What would the Border raiders do now? Oh, yes——'

Once again she was swept into his arms as though she weighed nothing at all. From the rug, Cleo watched, then sighed and stretched her muzzle on her paws.

'Adam, where are we going?'

'Where do you think, my love?' His eyes travelled over her slowly, deliciously, with a look so intense that she could sense it on her skin. Then he grinned. 'I hope I can negotiate the narrow staircase like this—it's very unromantic.'

'Adam—put me down.'

'You don't think I'm going to let you go now that I've finally found you, do you? Oh, Jessica——' his voice was suddenly thick with longing, the teasing note gone. 'You don't know how much I've wanted you!'

'Adam—put me down. I want to talk to you.'

'But——' Then he sighed, and did as he was told. 'You'd better have something worthwhile to say.'

'I do. Adam, I'm going to get tidied up, and I'm going to find a pair of shoes, and then we're going to tell your father about us.'

He stared at her, dismayed. 'Now?'

'Now.'

He reached out for her, shaped her shoulders, back, and waist with tender, loving hands. 'Afterwards,' he suggested.

'Now.' She stopped his protests with a finger on his lips. 'This is a special moment for us both. I'm not Kate, remember? I'm Jessica. And I'm going to break the Brodie legend, once and for all.'

He caught at her hand, kissed it, then looked at the ring on her finger. 'You're wearing Kate's friendship ring.'

'I thought it was time for it to be worn again, after all. It brought her happiness—and it brought us together tonight, when it was almost too late for us both. Adam, I want to be sure of my man. I want him to be mine—not just to have a share in his life, as Kate had with Edward.'

'You can be sure!' he promised her huskily. She looked up at him, and knew, by the love in the eyes holding hers, that this time the bubble of happiness surrounding them wouldn't burst.

'My love, I want everyone to know that we belong to each other.'

'Jessica——' he cupped her chin in his hand, then his fingers strayed to the nape of her neck, drawing her against his shoulder. 'Do you know how much I want you? Do you know how long I've waited for you to come into my life?'

'I know,' she said breathlessly against his smooth, warm throat. 'But what about the Brodie women?'

'The—what?'

'The Brodie women. You all make such a fuss about the men. What about the women? What about me? I'm going to put an end to that nonsense about the Brodie men straying. You're going to be trapped with me for always—for all the time that will ever be, my darling. Because I'm going to marry you, as soon as my parents get here, next month. And before that—tonight, in fact—I'm going to ask your father if he would be willing to have that lovely old house turned back into one lovely old house. You see? I'm going to change your life, and then you won't be able to get me out of it easily!'

He threw his head back and laughed. 'I thought lawyers were supposed to be practical,' he accused. 'But you take the biscuit! I have a strong feeling, Jessica, that you're going to be good for me!'

She looked into his brown eyes, letting herself drown in the wonderful future they promised her.

'We're going to be good for each other,' she promised him. 'Oh, we're going to be very good for each other, Adam Brodie!' A P